Fairy Tale Time

Retold by Jane Carruth

TREASURE PRESS

Contents

First published in Great Britain by Octopus Books Ltd

This edition published by Treasure Press
59 Grosvenor Street
London W1

Original edition © 1976 Fabbri Editori, Milan
This edition © 1979 Octopus Books Ltd

ISBN 0 907407 99 4

Printed in Czechoslovakia

50499

The illustrations were drawn by the following artists:
Barilli: pages 190–208
Ferri: pages 6–25; 90–103
Lima: pages 118–141; 166–189
Max: pages 26–49
Pinardi: pages 142–165
Sergio: pages 115–117
Una: pages 50–65
Violetto: pages 66–89

The Sleeping Beauty

Once upon a time there lived a king and queen who wished with all their hearts to have a child.

They consulted all the wise women in their kingdom; they made long and very difficult pilgrimages to distant lands, and they gave huge sums of money to charity in the hope that one day their dream would come true.

Well, that day came at last. The queen gave birth to a pretty baby daughter, and the king and his subjects rejoiced in her happiness.

'We must give a party for our darling child,' the queen said one morning as she sat at breakfast with the king. 'We have not yet named our daughter, so it will be a christening party.'

'A christening party is a splendid idea!' exclaimed the king. 'What name shall we give our child?'

'I have been wondering about that,' his wife said. 'What do you think of Floratina or perhaps Rosabella?'

'Let us call her Rosabella,' said the king, after a moment's thought. 'It is a pretty name and it brings to mind the beauty of our rose garden.'

The queen was delighted that her husband should agree so willingly to the name of her choice and she went on to discuss the plans she had for the grand christening party, and the guests they should invite.

'All our friends at court must receive invitations,' she said eagerly. 'And we must not forget the good fairies. They will be our most important guests for, as you know, they may bestow upon our precious child the special gifts which only fairies have the power to give.'

'Certainly the good fairies must be invited,' the king agreed. 'And what is more, I suggest that we have something unusual in the way of presents prepared for them. I will order a golden casket for each of them . . .'

'Yes, yes,' interrupted the queen, 'and we could put something useful inside. I think a knife and fork and spoon with beautiful jewelled handles would be most acceptable to the fairies.'

'I will see to it immediately,' the king promised as he finished his breakfast. 'I will see that the caskets are ready in time for the christening party.'

The queen spent the rest of the morning sending out personal invitations to the christening. She consulted her ladies-in-waiting about the lists of guests to be invited and she went so far as to write a short friendly note to each of the good fairies, some of whom lived many hundreds of leagues from the palace, in which she said their presence at the party would give her the greatest joy and happiness. Then, as soon as all the invitations were sent out, she hurried to the royal nursery where her lovely baby daughter lay in her cradle. She was soon joined by the king, and the royal parents spent a happy hour with their child.

It had been decided to hold the grand christening party within one week, and the news spread throughout the land. The king's subjects, from the highest to the lowest, sent gifts to the princess, and the high-born ladies who had received invitations to the christening party kept their dressmakers very busy.

On the great day itself the palace was bustling with activity. Servants ran hither and thither carrying out their orders, and in the magnificent banqueting hall places were laid for each of the guests at long tables which were richly decorated in silver and gold.

At the top table at which the king and queen would sit were the places for the good fairies. Their golden caskets

The king and queen spent a happy hour with their baby daughter.

The little princess lay happily in the lap of her grandmother.

gleamed in the sunlight and the queen, who had found time to take a quick glance round the banqueting hall, was quite delighted with them.

'The fairies will love the caskets,' she whispered to the king as the first guests began to arrive. 'I am so pleased we thought of giving them special gifts.'

The little princess lay gurgling happily in the lap of her grandmother as the admiring guests gathered round. The proud and happy parents were content to remain in the background, listening to the compliments which their friends showered upon their baby daughter.

When the moment came for the presentation of the gifts, the good fairies clearly had something very special in mind for the royal baby. But, alas, before they could step forward an ugly and sneering chuckle broke through the happy laughter that filled the room. It came from an aged fairy, with sharp glinting eyes and long hooked nose.

All but one of the good fairies bestowed their magic gifts upon the little princess.

'She shall have beauty.'

'Laugh! Laugh!' she screeched, pointing a bony finger at the assembled guests. 'But I will not laugh with you. I am the guest that was forgotten . . .'

'Gracious!' the queen whispered to her husband. 'It is true what she says—I did not send her an invitation!'

As she spoke, all but one of the good fairies came forward to bestow their magic gifts upon the little princess.

'She shall have beauty,' said one.

'And dance and sing divinely,' said another.

'She will be as wise as she is lovely,' said the third.

'She will be gifted at music,' said the fourth.

'She will be so gentle and kind that all will love her,' said the fifth.

'And dance and sing divinely.'

'She will be as wise as she is lovely.'
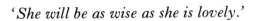

The aged fairy hobbled into view with a menacing glance.

'She will be full of grace,' said the sixth.

The king and queen smiled happily as one by one the fairies came forward. Indeed they had forgotten all about the aged crone. But not so the youngest of the good fairies, who had remained hidden behind one of the pillars in order to keep a watchful eye on the spiteful old hag.

Presently as the good fairies retired, the aged fairy hobbled into view. With a menacing glance at the royal parents, she croaked, 'You have hurriedly laid a place for me at your feast but where is the gold casket which, by rights, is mine?'

'We—we did not remember,' stammered the queen, suddenly unhappy and afraid. 'I—I—that is—there is no golden casket for you . . .'

'You have no gift for me but I have one for that precious babe of yours!' the old fairy shrieked. 'Oh yes, she will have all the grace and beauty in the world. But I tell you she will never grow to womanhood. She will die—die from the prick of a spindle when she is but fifteen years old! There—you have my gift.'

At this the youngest of the good fairies appeared from behind the pillar. 'She will not die,' she said firmly. 'She will simply fall into a deep sleep which will last one hundred years. The kiss of a young prince will rouse her from this sleep. This is my gift.'

The king and queen took comfort from the good fairy's words. But that same day the king sent out his heralds with a warning to his subjects. They must burn all their spinning wheels on pain of death.

'It is the king's most solemn command,' the heralds told the people. 'So pay heed to it!'

The king's heralds warned that all spinning wheels must be burned.

The royal procession set out to visit a country castle which belonged to the king.

As the years passed, the evil fairy's curse on the princess was almost forgotten. Rosabella was the prettiest, kindest girl imaginable and so graceful and with so many wonderful gifts that her parents and the entire court loved her dearly. They were forever trying to think up some new pleasure for her and one day, in the heat of the summer, the king suggested that they all go on a visit to one of his country castles.

'You will enjoy the ancient old castle,' he told his daughter. 'And so too will some of our faithful attendants. We shall all have a splendid holiday there.'

The royal procession set out the next day. The tall grey castle set on a high high hill was so different from the palace that the princess vowed she loved it on sight because it seemed so romantic.

'Let us hope it is comfortable,' said the queen. 'It is many, many years since we have visited it.'

That night, as the princess and her parents settled into their summer home, there was feasting and dancing, and Rosabella said that in the morning she would explore the old castle from turret to cellar.

'It is a great pity that you have so few young companions of your own age to amuse you,' said the queen, with a loving glance at her slim, golden-haired daughter. 'But we shall arrange some hunting parties and your father has promised that I may hold a ball for you.'

Rosabella's fair young face lit up as she listened to her mother's plans for her. She was fifteen years old now and so very beautiful and gracious that there was hardly a young man at court who had not vowed to die for her. But, for the moment, she was so happy at home that she did not wish to encourage any suitors.

The old woman looked up in amazement at the sight of the pretty young girl, for it was many years since she had had a visitor. 'Why, Missy!' she cried. 'What brings you here? What do you want?'

'Want! Want!' laughed the princess. 'I want nothing of you, mother! But pray tell me what you are doing so busily! I declare I have never seen anything quite so odd in all my life!' And she laughed and then clapped her hands. 'Let me try, please, I would so much like to . . .'

'Why, child, don't you know I am spinning,' said the old woman. 'In my young day every woman and child knew

She asked the old woman what she was doing.

She came upon the steep narrow stairs that led to the tower.

Next morning, long before her parents were up, Rosabella set out to explore the castle. Almost immediately she came upon the steep narrow stairs that led to the tower and she climbed them quickly, her light steps making no sound.

The rooms at the top of the castle were bare and empty—that is all except one, which was lit by shafts of light coming through the narrow slits that served as windows.

For a moment Rosabella thought she was alone, until she spied an old dame seated at an empty hearth and busily engaged in some strange work.

Rosabella pricked her finger on the spindle.

what to do with a spindle . . .' and she sighed for it was a long, long time since she had been a child.

'A spindle—is that what you call that thing in your hand?' cried the young princess. 'Here—give it to me—let me try to . . .'

And she ran to the old dame and took hold of the spindle.

Now, who can say if the wicked fairy's cruel powers were already at work? And that what happened next was meant to be! Rosabella held the spindle so awkwardly that it slipped and pricked her finger.

With the faintest sigh she fell to the ground and lay there as one dead.

The old woman cried out in alarm and hurried to the door to shout for help. When the king and queen came rushing up the steep stairs and saw their beautiful child lying so still on the hard stone floor, they broke out into sobs.

Then the king said, 'The old witch has had her way. We know our daughter will not wake up for a hundred years.'

And the queen tearfully begged him to send for the youngest fairy so that she might advise them what to do.

Urgent messages were then despatched to the fairy. Her arrival at the castle in a fiery chariot drawn by a dragon put new courage into the king and his lords, but she could offer little comfort. 'Let the princess sleep on a bed of silver and gold,' she said. 'She will be as fair and lovely in sleep—though it lasts one hundred years—as she is now. And she will not find herself among strange faces

The whole castle fell into a deep sleep.

A thick briar hedge sprung up around the castle.

when she awakes, for I will send all her ladies-in-waiting, the castle servants, the dogs, cats and all the horses in the stables into a sleep which will hold them bound for a hundred years.'

The good fairy then bade the king and queen kiss their daughter farewell as she set about her work. At the touch of her wand the cook, as he raised his tasting ladle to his mouth, was overcome by sleep. The naughty little kitchen-maid who was teasing the cat instantly fell asleep as the fairy touched her. So too did all the lords and ladies of the palace, and the merry court jesters.

Outside in the courtyard the king's favourite hunting hound sank to the ground and lay motionless. And the horses slept where they stood while the stable-boys lay on the ground or leaned against the walls with their eyes closed.

Then, as the king and queen rode sadly away in their coach, the fairy caused a thick briar hedge to spring up all around the castle before she too departed.

Countless legends were told of the old

grey castle which, with the passing of years, was scarcely visible behind its dense barrier of thorny shrubs and twisted gnarled trees. And many a daring young adventurer tried to hack his way through the forbidding hedge in an effort to reach the castle and find out if it was really true that a beautiful princess lay fast asleep inside.

One day a brave young prince came into the forest. He had been riding hard all morning and had left his retainers far behind. As he dismounted, he caught a fleeting glimpse of the tall grey castle set on a hill and protected by its hedge of briars. Turning to an old woodcutter, who was busy with his axe, he demanded to be told about the mysterious castle.

'I would that I could tell you, sire,' mumbled the old man. 'All I know for

The tangled hedge parted before the prince.

certain is that it's a hundred years since there was any sign of life there.'

'But that is most interesting!' cried the prince. 'What else can you tell me, old man? Come, I will reward you.'

'My great-grandmother used to tell us boys about a beautiful princess who is supposed to lie asleep inside the castle,' went on the woodcutter. 'But there is likely to be very little truth in such a tale.'

'Oh, I don't know about that!' the prince said quietly. 'It would be worth finding out though.'

'Do not attempt to break through that briar hedge,' warned the old man. 'I've reason to know that two or three of the village lads have been torn to pieces when they tried to.'

The young prince laughed and drew his sword. 'Well, perhaps I shall fare better!' he cried, and ran forward.

To his surprise as he approached the tangled hedge with its terrible thorns, it parted before him, and he was able to go forward without any hindrance.

'This is the beginning of a very strange adventure,' he told himself, as he set off along the narrow path that wound its way upwards through the dead, twisted branches of stunted trees.

Now he could see the whole castle and his determination grew as he pressed on towards the mysterious place. He'd find out for himself the truth of the legend!

When at last he reached the huge iron gates and entered the courtyard, he saw to his amazement the sleeping grooms and the horses. For a moment he wondered whether the ferocious hound which sprawled on the stones would rise up and attack him. But like the other animals the hound lay motionless, its eyes closed in slumber.

With a sigh of relief the prince ran on and was soon in the castle itself. How eerily silent it was! And how strange to come upon so many servants sound asleep —some still holding their brushes, others in the very act of scrubbing floors.

'This place is under some enchantment,' the prince told himself, as he wandered from one room to the next. 'Now I am ready to believe that sooner or later I shall come upon the beautiful princess that the old woodcutter told me about . . .'

Long and diligently he searched the castle, hoping against hope for some sign of life. But there were only the spiders and their cobwebs and the thick grey dust in the passageways.

At the end of one of the longest corridors he came at last to a door, which opened on to a room a hundred times more richly furnished than any of the others.

And there on a bed of silver and gold lay the most beautiful girl the prince had ever set eyes on.

Her eyes were closed in sleep, but her skin was as soft and blooming as if only yesterday the sun had kissed her delicate cheeks.

She was so lovely that the prince caught his breath in wonder and then, tiptoeing up to the bed, he bent over and gently placed a kiss upon her rose-tinted lips.

At the touch of his kiss the princess stirred and opened her eyes. Then, with

On a bed of silver and gold lay the most beautiful girl the prince had ever set eyes on.

no hint of surprise or fear in her voice, she whispered, 'So you have come!' And she sat up in bed, holding out her arms to the young man who stood over her.

The prince held her for a moment before saying, 'Tell me who you are? Are you truly the enchanted princess of the legend.'

'I think I must be,' smiled the princess. 'And you are the prince who, one hundred years to the day, has broken the spell which a wicked fairy cast upon me.'

As she spoke, the castle came to life. In the kitchens the cook raised his tasting ladle to his lips and pronounced the soup quite excellent. The naughty little kitchen-maid pulled the cat's tail, the lords and ladies completed their letter-writing and their singing lessons, and the scullery-maids their scrubbing.

And out in the courtyard the hounds bayed, the cats miaowed, and the horses tossed their heads and neighed loudly for after one hundred years they wanted the attention of their grooms.

Two of the princess's ladies-in-waiting rushed into her room to brush her long hair and send the young prince packing until their royal mistress was properly dressed.

And the prince laughingly agreed to wait in the hall. 'I shall find the chaplain,' he told the ladies. 'And make arrangements for our wedding. It seems I have waited all my life for this wonderful day.'

The prince came upon the old chaplain just as he was getting up from one of the chapel's benches where indeed he had been seated for a hundred years! So it is no wonder he grumbled a little at the stiffness of his joints.

'Do not waste your breath on such matters,' said the prince. 'You are in very good shape, Father, considering you have been sitting here for a hundred years! Come, I will assist you to the castle with all speed, for you have a wedding ceremony to perform.'

And as they crossed the courtyard, arm in arm, the prince told the old man of his love for the Sleeping Beauty—the princess who had been waiting for him for so long.

In the meantime the princess, her blue eyes sparkling with happiness, was deep in consultation with her ladies-in-waiting as to which of her gowns she should wear.

Never had she looked more beautiful as she tried on first one and then a second and a third.

It is true that every dress in her wardrobe was a hundred years out of date, but when at length she was dressed, there was no one to tell her how fashions had changed over the years!

'The handsome prince will love you a thousand times more than he does already,' declared the youngest of her attendants as she swept out of the room. And the princess truly believed this as she ran down the stairs to find him.

He was waiting for her in the vast hall with the chaplain at his side. The holy man fussed a little and hummed a psalm under his breath to give himself time to remember just exactly how the marriage service was conducted. But the princess, who had known him all her life, begged him to hurry and make all the arrangements as fast as possible.

'You can see we are meant for each other,' she told the chaplain. 'Please see to it that the chapel is dusted and the cassocks made ready for I mean to marry my prince today.'

'I am already dressed for our wedding,'

she explained, turning to the prince and giving him a brilliant smile. And the young man told her how lovely she looked— though privately he thought it strange that she should have chosen to wear a gown with long tight sleeves.

You see, being a man of fashion, he knew very well that all the high-born ladies that year were wearing hooped dresses with very full sleeves!

Wisely, however, he remained silent on the subject of dress, and the radiant princess continued to think that she was dressed in the height of fashion.

The chaplain pulled himself together remarkably quickly. He had the chapel cleared of cobwebs and the cassocks dusted and placed in position.

He found his little black book which contained the marriage ceremony, and he read it through twice so that he would be word perfect when the time came.

And that very day, just as the two loving young people had wished, the wedding ceremony took place.

Afterwards the castle rang with the sound of happy laughter, as the guests celebrated the event. They were not guests in the proper sense of the word. They were the lords and ladies and all the servants who had fallen under the good fairy's spell. Even the naughty little kitchen-maid was present, and the two scullery-maids who had worked so hard to scrub the passageways before the ceremony.

And if you are wondering why the prince did not immediately take the young princess back to his own kingdom and to his palace, which was certainly grander than the castle—I'll tell you. He did not wish to share his Sleeping Beauty with anyone—not even his own family—until he had made her his wife!

After the wedding there was a great celebration.

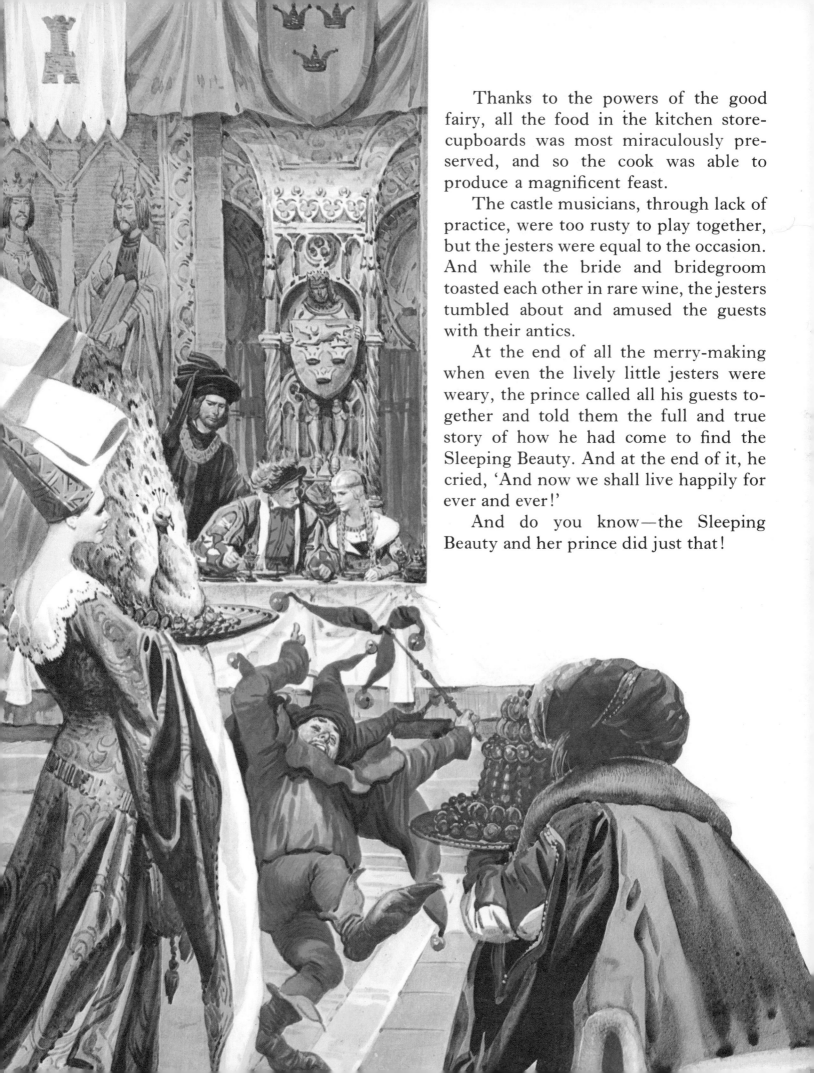

Thanks to the powers of the good fairy, all the food in the kitchen store-cupboards was most miraculously preserved, and so the cook was able to produce a magnificent feast.

The castle musicians, through lack of practice, were too rusty to play together, but the jesters were equal to the occasion. And while the bride and bridegroom toasted each other in rare wine, the jesters tumbled about and amused the guests with their antics.

At the end of all the merry-making when even the lively little jesters were weary, the prince called all his guests together and told them the full and true story of how he had come to find the Sleeping Beauty. And at the end of it, he cried, 'And now we shall live happily for ever and ever!'

And do you know—the Sleeping Beauty and her prince did just that!

Jack and the Beanstalk

Once upon a time there was a young widow woman who had a son called Jack, and a pretty cow called Daisy Belle. The widow was young enough to wish for money to spend on her son and on herself. Alas, after the death of her husband, it was all she could do to find the money for the rent. Like all good mothers she tried to keep her worries to herself, but Jack always knew when the rent was due.

'Let me go into the town,' he said to her one morning. 'I know I'm not very old, but surely one of the farmers who comes to market will give me a job.'

'No, no, Jack,' said his mother. 'You are too young. Besides I need you to help me here. And what about Daisy Belle?'

'What about Daisy Belle!' cried Jack. 'She's clever enough to find her own way back from the meadow at milking time.'

'You're probably right,' his mother said. 'She is the finest cow around and I don't know what we would do without her milk. But all the same she knows and trusts you . . .'

'You just want to keep me at home,' said Jack in a good-natured way. 'But I hate to see you begin to worry as soon as the time comes to send off the rent. Why don't we ask the landlord to wait a little while for it this time?'

'Perhaps I will,' sighed his mother. 'If you really think he will pay attention to a letter . . .'

'I'm sure he will,' said Jack.

So the widow sat down and wrote a few lines to her landlord, asking for more time to pay. But the landlord wrote back by return saying that he was sorry but he was very hard-up and must have the money when it was due.

'Now what shall we do?' Jack's mother cried. 'The landlord means what he says. He won't give us any more time and we have only a few weeks left.'

Jack shook his head. He knew how his mother loved their cottage and what a blow it would be to her if they had to leave. He longed to be able to help, but his head was filled with dreams of finding a pot of gold at the bottom of the garden. There was nothing he could think of now that would help them to make some money to pay the rent.

'Perhaps Daisy Belle will give us so much milk tomorrow that we can sell it to our neighbours,' he suggested at last. 'And I could see if the hens have laid any eggs this morning.'

'Milk! Eggs!' his mother sighed. 'We need real money, Jack! And we need it very quickly.'

'If only I was a man!' Jack exclaimed. And he ran off into the meadows so that his mother would not see how unhappy he was.

The sight of Daisy Belle comforted him. There was something about her large liquid brown eyes and her gentle way of moving around the meadow that cheered Jack, and he began to tell himself that things couldn't be so bad.

'Something nice will happen soon,' Jack thought. 'The landlord won't take our cottage, even if we don't pay the rent, and he's not going to have our Daisy Belle or our hens . . .'

But, oh dear, later that day when he

Daisy Belle lived in the meadow near the house.

'We must sell the cow,' said his mother.

came home for his dinner, he found his
mother in her favourite rocking chair and
looking sadder than ever.

'Jack, come and listen to me,' she
began softly. And as Jack knelt beside her
chair, she went on, 'I have made up my
mind. I know what we must do. We must
sell the cow. It is the only way!'

'What!' Jack cried in distress. 'Oh, you
can't do that, Mother! You can't.'

He walked slowly along the road which led to the town.

'I'm sorry, Jack,' his mother said. 'I know what she means to you. She's a fine cow and we have had her a long time. But she will fetch a good price at the market, and we need the money for the rent. You must set off early in the morning with her. Take her straight to the market-place. I will have to trust you to make the best bargain you can.'

Well, Jack begged and pleaded with his mother to change her mind, but nothing he could say, not even his promise to try and find some work, was of any use.

The next morning he awoke early and his mother was waiting for him as he went down to breakfast.

'Remember, Jack,' she said, 'You must not sell her to the first farmer who comes along. You must be smart, as your father would have been, and wait until you get several offers. Then choose the best.'

'Don't worry,' said Jack, trying to sound cheerful. 'I'll make a very good bargain and then all our troubles will be over.'

He was thinking about his mother's advice as he set off with Daisy Belle for the market. But as he walked slowly along the road which led to the town, he could not help feeling terribly sad. He would miss Daisy Belle more perhaps than she would miss him. But at least he would make certain that he sold her to a kind farmer who would take good care of her.

Just as he drew near to the town, Jack was surprised to be saluted by an old man seated at the side of the road.

'Where are you off to, my lad?' asked the stranger with a smile.

'To market,' said Jack. 'I'm going to sell our cow.'

'Sell her to me,' said the stranger. 'Here take this bag of beans for her. They are magic and will make your fortune. Trust me, lad! I know what I'm talking about.'

'Magic beans! Make my fortune! Why,

'Take this bag of beans,' said the stranger.

sir that would be wonderful! Yes, please,
I'll take them in exchange for Daisy Belle.'

'Be sure to plant them this very night.
In the morning they will be up to the sky,'
said the old man.

Well, you can just imagine what Jack's
mother had to say when he showed her
the bag of magic beans. 'Look!' he
shouted, 'I'm to plant them tonight. Are
they not better than any money a farmer
could give us for Daisy Belle?'

*'How can we pay the rent with a bag of useless
beans?'*

His mother sent him to bed without any supper.

At first she was too angry and too disappointed even to be able to cry. She stared at Jack and then she gasped, 'You talk about an old man and magic beans! I cannot believe my ears. Fool! Stupid, stupid fool! How can we pay the rent with a bag of useless beans?'

And she snatched the bag from Jack and threw it out of the window. The beans, all the colours of the rainbow, scattered on the brown earth and lay there, for-

gotten, as the angry widow went on scolding her stupid son.

'There will be no supper for you!' she stormed. 'You will go to bed hungry, and in the morning you must find that wicked old man and make him give you back the cow. Then you can take her to market, as you were meant to do, and get a fair price for her! Now off to bed with you!'

Poor Jack! As he climbed sadly up to bed, he thought of all the wonderful plans he had made when he was running home with the beans. Was his mother right after all? Had the old man cheated him just because he was still a boy?

Holding back his tears he undressed slowly and got into bed. His mother had said that he must find the old man in the morning. But where was he going to look? He had never seen him before and when he had turned back to wave, he wasn't there. The old man and Daisy Belle had completely vanished as if the ground had swallowed them up!

For a long time Jack lay wide awake. If he didn't find Daisy Belle and take her to market, they would have no money for the rent. They might have to leave their cottage, which would break his mother's heart.

'It will all be my fault,' he thought, as he tossed and turned in bed. 'She will always say it was my fault.'

For a long time Jack lay wide awake.

When sleep came at last, Jack began to dream. At one time he was running along the road, scattering the brightly coloured beans. Red, blue, green and purple—they lay like pretty beads on the brown earth!

'They are magic, I tell you!' Jack heard himself say. 'Magic, magic, magic! They will grow up and up into the sky. I know they will. I don't believe the old man was trying to cheat me!'

The dream was so vivid that he woke up and lay quite still for some time, trying to remember it.

When he closed his eyes again he dreamed he was walking slowly along a white road and there at the end of it was the old man waiting for him.

'Good boy, Jack,' said the old man and his voice was kind. 'Good boy!'

'Don't go away!' Jack heard himself shout. 'Tell me what you have done with Daisy Belle! You must give her back to

Jack dreamed of the old man.

me. It has been a horrible mistake. Tell me where to find her.'

'Trust me, Jack,' said the old man. 'Soon it will be morning. Then you will see your magic beans towering upwards into the blue sky.'

As Jack reached out in his dream to grasp hold of the old man, he woke up. It was morning, and there outside the window were the giant leaves of what appeared to be an enormous beanstalk!

'It's true after all!' Jack gasped. 'The

There outside the window were the giant leaves of an enormous beanstalk!

beans were magic, and when Mother threw them away, they must have taken root in our garden and just grown and grown . . .'

Scarcely daring to believe his eyes, he jumped out of bed and peered at the giant beanstalk through the open window.

There it was, reaching straight up into the sky, just as the old man had said it

Jack jumped out of bed and peered at the giant beanstalk.

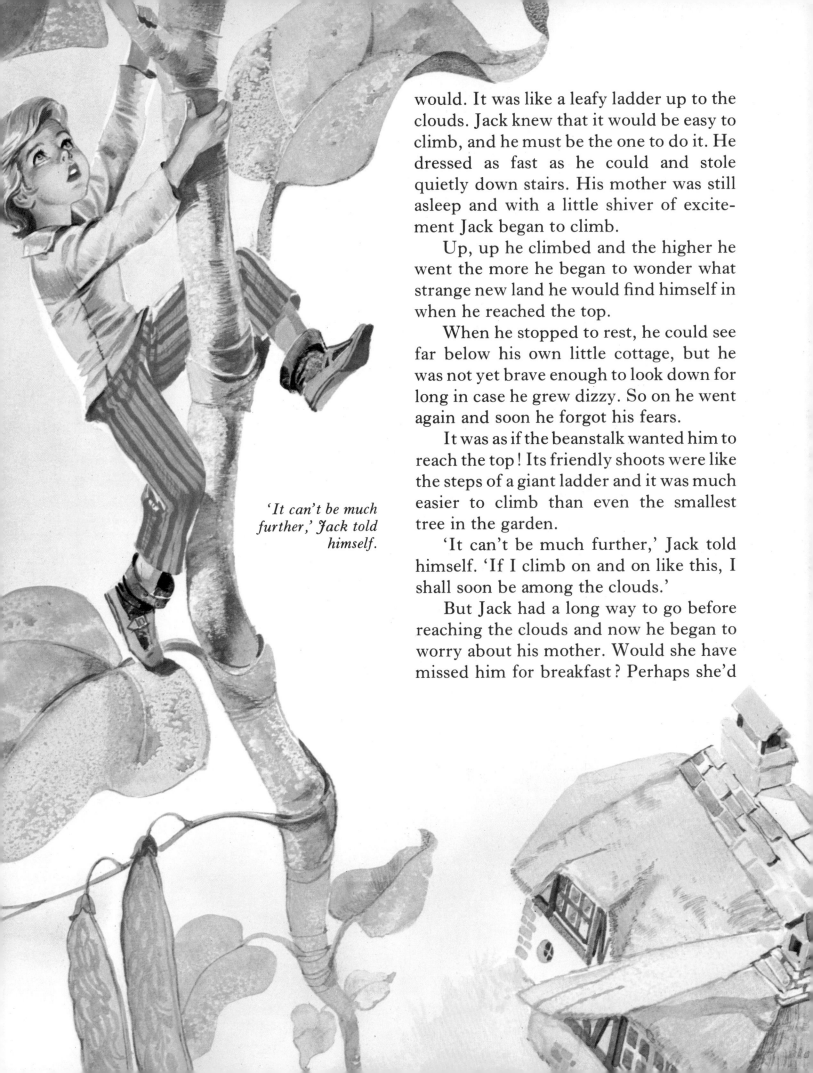

would. It was like a leafy ladder up to the clouds. Jack knew that it would be easy to climb, and he must be the one to do it. He dressed as fast as he could and stole quietly down stairs. His mother was still asleep and with a little shiver of excitement Jack began to climb.

Up, up he climbed and the higher he went the more he began to wonder what strange new land he would find himself in when he reached the top.

When he stopped to rest, he could see far below his own little cottage, but he was not yet brave enough to look down for long in case he grew dizzy. So on he went again and soon he forgot his fears.

It was as if the beanstalk wanted him to reach the top! Its friendly shoots were like the steps of a giant ladder and it was much easier to climb than even the smallest tree in the garden.

'It can't be much further,' Jack told himself. 'If I climb on and on like this, I shall soon be among the clouds.'

But Jack had a long way to go before reaching the clouds and now he began to worry about his mother. Would she have missed him for breakfast? Perhaps she'd

'It can't be much further,' Jack told himself.

think he had already left to find the old
man and Daisy Belle. What would she say
when he saw her again? Would she be
sorry that she had poured such scorn on
his magic beans? He hoped she would.

Jack was so busy trying to find all the
answers to his questions that he did not
pause or look down until he was high up
on the beanstalk.

And then, with a shock, he saw how
tiny the houses were below, like little
cardboard models.

'Goodness! I really am among the
clouds,' he thought, as he clung to the
beanstalk. 'It can't be very much further.'

He was tired now and no longer feeling
very brave. He tried to think of the old
man's smiling face and he told himself all
over again that his beans were magic and

*He saw how tiny the houses
were below, like little
cardboard models.*

that the old man had wished him well, and had not tried to cheat him.

As he rested, the swirling clouds all about him suddenly cleared and he saw, to his amazement, a great tall castle rising out of them.

Suddenly all his fears were forgotten as he gazed at the castle. He saw that a broad white road led from his beanstalk to the great house, and his heart thudded with excitement. He would leave the beanstalk and take the road ahead!

Soon he was running along the road towards the castle. Up the broad steps he went, without pausing for breath, and through the half-open door.

'Is there anyone there?' he shouted.

And presently a great tall woman came into the dark hall. She stared down at him and then asked in a voice that was not un-friendly, 'What do you want, boy?'

'Please, ma'am,' said Jack, 'would you be kind enough to give me some break-fast? I've come ever such a long way and I'm so hungry I could eat a whole loaf of bread.' Then he added after a pause, 'I won't be a nuisance . . .'

'You poor lamb,' said the great tall woman. 'You poor lamb! Do you know who owns this castle?'

'No, ma'am,' said Jack, shaking his head. 'But he must be rich and important whoever he is to live in such a fine place.'

'This castle belongs to an ogre!' cried the woman. 'Oh yes, he's my husband, but if he knew I had invited you inside, I daren't think what he would do . . .'

'He doesn't eat little boys I don't suppose!' Jack laughed. 'So, if you don't mind, I'll take my chance.'

'Eat small boys — why, that is just what he does do, given the chance!' said the ogre's wife. 'But there may be time to give you a bit of breakfast before he returns from his walk.'

'That's very kind of you ma'am,' said Jack gratefully, as he followed the woman into a vast kitchen. 'Bread and cheese will do very nicely, thank you.'

Alas, Jack had scarcely begun the meal which the good woman set before him when there was a terrible noise, like the sound of runaway horses, and then the whole castle began to shake.

'Gracious me!' the woman exclaimed. 'My husband's coming back!' And she took the plate of bread and cheese and hid it in one of the cupboards. Then she turned to Jack. 'If he finds you here, he'll have you grilled on toast for his breakfast. Quick, hide in the oven!' And she pushed Jack into the huge oven and shut the door.

Well, she was only just in time. The ogre was in the room before she had even turned round. And what a dreadful fellow he was, with arms and legs like tree trunks and a voice like thunder.

He sniffed the air suspiciously as he strode into the room. Then he roared,
'Fee-fi-fo-fum!
I smell the blood of an Englishman
Be he alive or be he dead,
I'll grind his bones to make my bread!'

When Jack heard this cruel threat, he kept as still as a mouse inside the oven. Then he heard the ogre's wife say, 'Come, husband, it is only this roast sheep you smell. Sit down and eat while it is nice and hot.'

Well, the ogre was hungry and he was soon persuaded by his wife to start on his breakfast. When he had stuffed himself with the roast sheep and drunk four bottles of dark red wine, he called for his bags of

He saw a great tall castle rising out of the clouds.

'Is there anyone
there?'

gold. For a time he kept himself very happily occupied by counting all the coins they contained, but presently he grew tired and sleepy, and he put his great head down on the table and was soon fast asleep and snoring loudly.

As soon as Jack heard the loud snores, he crept out of the oven, snatched one of the bags of gold and made off. Down the beanstalk he scrambled and on reaching the bottom began shouting for his mother.

'Mother! Mother! Come and see what I have brought you!'

The poor woman was overcome at the sight of the giant's gold.

'Our troubles are over!' she cried in a thankful voice. 'Now we can pay all the rent for years to come.'

'The old man was my friend after all,' said Jack, as he followed her into the cottage. 'And the beans are magic!'

Well, Jack and his mother lived in comfort for some time. But, to their surprise, the gold did not last nearly as long as they had hoped.

'I'll just climb the beanstalk once more,' Jack said to his mother one evening.

'I may be lucky again.'

Jack snatched one of the bags of gold and made off.

'Lay me some of your golden eggs, my pretty hen!'

The ogre's wife was so surprised to see Jack a second time that she invited him in for a bowl of porridge. But no sooner had he started to eat than there was a loud thumping noise. The ogre was coming home! And without being told, Jack ran to the oven to hide.

As he entered the kitchen, the fierce ogre sniffed the air suspiciously, but his wife hurriedly placed an enormous dish of roast meat before him.

'Eat up, husband,' she said. 'And then you can have your magic hen.'

'Magic hen?' Jack wondered. 'Now what is magic about a hen?'

He was soon to find out, for presently he heard the ogre exclaim, 'Lay me some of your golden eggs, my pretty hen!'

When the ogre's loud snores told Jack it was safe, he crept from his hiding-place and picked up the magic hen. The hen set up a shrill cackling and he put her in a sack, hoping the noise would not disturb the sleeping giant.

But, oh dear, the ogre did wake up!

'Stop thief! Stop thief!' he roared, from the window.

He picked up the magic hen.

'Stop thief! Stop thief!'

With the sack over his shoulder the boy began scrambling down the beanstalk, before the ogre came along.

So, for the second time, Jack was able to tell his mother that he had outwitted the terrible ogre.

'This magic hen will lay us eggs of solid gold,' he assured her. 'And we shall get a lot of money for them. Our worries are over.'

But as time passed, Jack began to wish for just one more adventure, for the beanstalk was still there in the garden.

'It will be my last climb,' he said to his mother one day. 'Give me your blessing for I mean to climb that beanstalk just once more.'

And seeing that nothing she could say would change her son's mind, the widow gave him her blessing.

Early the next morning Jack climbed the beanstalk for the third time. When he reached the castle, he did not ask the ogre's wife to let him in. Instead he entered the kitchen by a small window he had spied on his last visit. Then he hid away in an empty chest that stood in a corner of the room.

It was dark and warm inside the chest and Jack settled down to wait for the ogre. He came almost at once—thump, thump, thump, across the kitchen floor—and the castle shook under his heavy step.

'Wife!' he roared. 'Can that rascally boy be here? Fee-fi-fo-fum—I smell the blood of . . .'

'You smell nothing but your food,' said his wife sharply. 'The lad is not here.' And she crossed to the oven and peered inside. 'I tell you he isn't here!'

After the ogre had eaten enough for ten men he called, 'Bring me my little singing harp.'

And his wife placed on the table before him a tiny golden harp.

'Harp, sing for me!' ordered the giant, and the harp began to sing.

So beautiful were its songs that Jack almost wept for joy as he listened, and he made up his mind to take the harp.

He waited until the ogre was lulled to sleep by the harp's sweet singing, and then he crept from his hiding-place and ran to the table. The ogre was sleeping so deeply that Jack was able to put the tiny harp in its blue silken bag before making off with it. But as he fled from the room, the harp cried loudly, 'Master! Master!'

Up sprang the ogre in a terrible rage and though Jack was running faster than ever before, the ogre was almost at his heels as he reached the beanstalk.

Down he scrambled, still clutching his precious burden, and after him came the furious ogre. But the ogre was big and heavy and clumsy, and nimble Jack was at the foot of the beanstalk when he was only half way down.

'Mother, Mother, bring the axe!' Jack shouted, and the widow came running and thrust the axe into his hand.

With all his strength Jack chopped away at the beanstalk until—crash—down it came, and the ogre with it. He hit the

Jack chopped away at the beanstalk until —crash—down it came, and the ogre with it.

ground with such a tremendous thud that it cracked wide open and swallowed him up!

So that was the end of the ogre and the wonderful beanstalk which had helped to make Jack's fortune.

With the magic hen to lay golden eggs whenever they needed money, and the little harp to sing to them in the long winter evenings, it is no wonder that Jack and his mother lived happily ever after!

The Frog Prince

A long, long time ago, when the world was young and fresh, there lived a king whose family were all very beautiful.

Portraits of his beautiful wife and daughters were to be seen everywhere in his splendid castle, and the king delighted in pointing them out to visitors, but especially the pictures of his youngest child, for she was the most lovely of his daughters.

The young princess had hair that shone like spun gold in the sunshine and a skin which was as soft and smooth as the petals of a rose. She was so beautiful that some said she outshone the sun itself, which will give you some idea of how she was admired by all who saw her.

The king was so proud of his youngest child that he gave her many precious toys and among them was a wonderful golden ball which the princess treasured above her other costly playthings.

Every day, when the sun was doing its best to outshine her beauty, which it never did, she would take her golden ball into the royal forest. This forest bounded the king's castle on three sides. It was a very ancient forest and it contained an old well by which the princess liked to sit in the sunshine.

One morning the princess went as usual into the forest to sit by the well. But after a time she grew tired of sitting still and she began playing with her precious golden ball.

She tossed it in the air, smiling with pleasure as it glinted in the sun, and as it fell, she caught it in both hands. The game she was playing with her golden ball was one she had often played. But this morning she began tossing it higher and higher into the air.

And then, oh dear, she threw the ball upwards once too often, for when it came down, she failed to catch it. The ball dropped into the well with a huge splash and sank like a stone!

The young princess gave a gasp of dismay as she knelt down by the ancient well. She hoped that she might catch a glimpse of her precious ball. But it was just as if the well had swallowed it up. There was no sign of it.

'What shall I do? What shall I do?' the princess wailed aloud. And she was so unhappy at the thought of losing her most precious plaything that she began to cry. She was sobbing so bitterly that she did not notice the big ugly frog which had hopped out of the well and was sitting in the grass beside her.

The frog seemed to be waiting for her to speak to him and when she paid him no attention, he said, 'What's the matter with you? Why are you crying as if your heart would break?'

'My beautiful golden ball has fallen into this old well,' the princess replied, when she had managed to stifle her sobs. 'I loved it so much and now it's lost and I won't ever see it again.'

'I live down that old well,' said the frog. 'I daresay I could find your ball and bring it back to you . . .'

At this the princess gave a final sniff and dried her eyes. 'You—you really think you could?' she exclaimed. 'Oh do please try, dear frog. I would be so grateful!'

'You would have to make it worth my while,' said the frog. 'What would you give me if I did you this favour?'

'Well, you see I am a princess,' the girl began. 'Do you know what that means?'

'I knew you were a princess,' answered

The golden ball fell into the well.

the frog. 'You didn't have to tell me. I have often watched you playing here.'

'Then you will know that I can give you anything you ask for,' said the princess with a smile. 'What would you suggest? I can bring you my little golden crown if you like next time I come to the forest.'

'No thank you,' said the frog.

'I have a casket of pearls and rubies,' said the princess. 'You may have the casket if you wish.'

'No, I don't want your casket,' said the frog.

'Then what do you want?' demanded the princess impatiently.

'I want to be your playmate,' said the frog. 'I want to be invited to stay in the castle and sit with you at meals. If you let me eat from your plate and sleep in your

*'I daresay I could find your ball and
bring it back to you . . .'*

little bed, then I will fetch the ball up
from the bottom of the well.'

'But that is perfectly ridiculous!' the
princess cried.

'If you say so,' replied the frog, and
he made as if he meant to jump back into
the well.

'Wait, wait!' the princess gasped. 'I will do as you say. You can be my very own playmate.' But even as she spoke she was thinking, 'Whoever heard of an ugly frog living in a castle? Once he fetches the ball I'll put him out of my mind.'

The frog did not guess what she was thinking and he hopped into the water and sank from sight.

The young princess clasped her hands, anxiously wondering if he would be clever enough to find her golden ball. And then she gave a shriek of joy when she spied the broad ugly face of the frog with the ball in his mouth. He swam to the edge of the well and hopped out, throwing the beautiful ball at her feet.

'Now carry me back to your castle,' said the frog.

But the princess shook her head as she picked up the ball. 'No, no, not today!' she murmured. 'But thank you very much for finding my plaything.'

And before the frog could remind her

She turned her back on him and set off through the forest.

of her promise, she turned her back on him and set off through the forest at a run, moving much too fast for the poor old frog.

'Wait, wait for me!' the frog cried in his ugly, hoarse voice. But the little princess did not even turn her head at the sound of his pleading croak.

'I do believe the silly creature meant what he said,' she thought, when at last she was safely home. 'I'll never play near that old well again for I don't ever want to set eyes on him.'

And she ran up to her own private room and put the golden ball in its special box by the window so that she could see how pretty it was in the sunlight. Soon, as she busied herself with brushing her soft hair, she had quite forgotten the frog.

But the next day as she sat down to dinner with her father the king, there sounded a dull flippety-flop on the stairs leading to the great door of the castle.

This dull flippety-flop noise was followed by a gentle knocking, and the king told the princess to go to the door and see who was outside.

As she ran to obey, she heard a voice crying, 'Youngest daughter of the king, let me in, let me in!'

The princess opened the door just a tiny crack, and when she saw the ugly old frog standing there on the step, she shut it again with all speed and ran back to the table.

'Who was it?' asked the king, as the princess sat down at her place and began eating from her little golden plate.

'Nothing—nobody,' she answered. 'It—it m-must have been the wind!'

But her father saw how the colour had fled from her cheeks and how, instead of eating properly, she toyed with her food, and so he asked again, 'Who was it, my child? Was it some terrible monster out there who frightened you?'

'No, no, not at all,' said the young princess. 'It was only a stupid ugly old frog. When I was playing by the well in the forest, I lost my golden ball. It fell into the water, and when I began crying at its loss, the frog offered to get it for me on condition that he became my little playmate. Why, he even made me promise to let him eat from my golden plate! It's really too ridiculous!' And the princess sniffed and tossed her head.

'It is not ridiculous,' said the king. 'You tell me you gave your promise to the frog. No daughter of mine must break her promise—even to a frog!'

Seeing the angry disappointed look on her father's face, the princess rose from the table and stood beside him. 'If I let the frog in,' she cried, 'he will try to sit at

'If I let the frog in,' she cried, 'he will try to sit at the table with me.'

table with me and eat from my golden plate.' And she pouted crossly.

'If that is what you promised him, then that is what you must permit him to do,' said the king. 'Now go to the door and invite the frog inside.'

The princess hesitated, but she did not dare disobey her father and slowly she went over to the door and opened it.

The frog hopped inside and followed her back to the table. Then he said, 'I want to eat with you, youngest daughter of the king. Lift me on to your lap.'

'Do as he says,' her father ordered, and the princess lifted the clammy frog on to her lap and he began eating from her own golden plate.

The poor princess could not swallow a single morsel of her dinner and presently she placed the frog on a high chair so that he might eat at his leisure while she sat beside him and watched.

The frog ate with delicate care the delicious food that was set before him, and the beautiful princess could not take her eyes from him. 'What a dreadful creature he is,' she thought. 'I wish he could fall from the table and vanish. I wish I had never asked him to get my ball. I wish . . .' She was so busy with her spiteful thoughts that she scarcely heard the frog's polite request to be lifted down.

When she paid no attention to her unwelcome guest, the frog repeated his wish in a much louder more demanding croak. 'I have eaten until I can eat no more,' he said. 'Lift me down from the king's table, my little princess, and carry me upstairs to your silken bed.'

'I won't—I will not!' exclaimed the princess indignantly. 'You shan't sleep in my bed!'

But the king said gently, 'Do as the frog asks, daughter. Remember your promise!'

And, after a moment's hesitation, the princess picked up the clammy frog and carried him up to her room.

'I hate you, you nasty creature,' she exclaimed, staring down at the frog, and she was ready to burst into tears. 'What can I do with you? How can I rid myself of you?'

And she put the frog in a corner of her bedroom as far away from her silken bed as she could. But the frog said, 'Lay me in your silken bed, princess, or I will tell your father.'

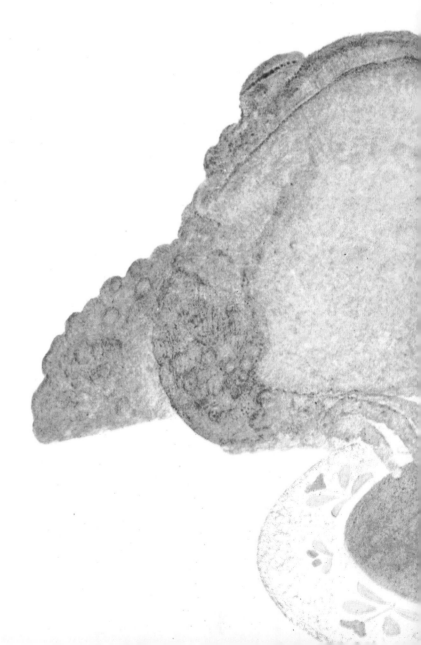

The princess could not take her eyes from him.

The frog changed into a tall noble young prince, richly clad in robes of silk.

The princess sobbed with anger and fear as once again she picked up the frog and carried him to her bed. Then, with a look of distaste, she put him between the silken sheets.

'Now climb in beside me,' said the frog. 'If you don't, I will tell the king.'

This was too much for the princess. With an angry scream she picked up the frog, and flung him with all her strength against the bedroom wall, at the same time crying, 'Hideous, horrible creature! I loathe and detest you . . .'

As she threw herself sobbing on the bed, something strange and wonderful took place. The frog, as he struck the wall, was no longer the clammy ugly creature he had been just seconds before, but a tall, noble young prince, richly clad in robes of silk.

The princess stared at the young man in amazement and, it must be confessed, in some shame. If she was to believe what her eyes were telling her, the handsome young man, with the kind friendly face, had once been a hideous frog. And she had treated the frog very shabbily!

'I—I am sorry . . .' she began. 'I—I did not guess . . .'

'You were not intended to,' said the prince with a smile. 'Some years ago a wicked fairy bewitched me and changed me into a frog. I was doomed to a life in the forest well until a lovely princess made me her guest . . .'

'But I didn't exactly do that,' put in the princess, blushing for shame.

'It was enough that you carried me to your room and with your own hands laid me in your bed,' said the prince. 'Now let us go together to your father, and ask him to allow us to marry.'

The princess was won over almost at once by the handsome prince who spoke with such kindness and she willingly agreed to ask her father's permission to marry him. This was given most willingly, for the king had only to look into the prince's eyes to see what a fine fellow he was.

The two young people then began making preparations for their wedding and on the day itself bells were rung from every church steeple announcing the happy event.

Never had the young princess looked more beautiful as she stood at the altar beside her handsome prince, and then indeed she did outshine the sun!

Early the next morning, when the pair were man and wife, there came to the castle a most magnificent coach to take the happy couple away to the prince's own

castle which stood in a neighbouring kingdom and which was even grander than the king's.

The coach was drawn by eight splendid white horses with coloured plumes fixed to their proud heads. At the back of it rode one of the prince's most faithful servants whose name was Henry.

When his master had been changed to a frog by the wicked fairy, the devoted Henry had three bands of iron placed around his heart so that it would not break from pity and grief.

The coach was drawn by eight splendid white horses with coloured plumes fixed to their proud heads.

Now, as the faithful servant assisted his royal master and the beautiful princess into the golden coach, there was the sound of splintering and cracking.

The princess looked round in alarm and the prince cried, 'Henry, Henry, is the coach safe to ride in?'

With a smile Henry replied,
'The bands from my heart have fallen in twain,
For long I suffered woe and pain.
While you a frog within a well
Enchanted by the witch's spell!'

And the Frog Prince gripped his loyal servant's hand before seating himself at the side of his new wife in the golden coach that was to carry them to their new home.

So ends the story of the beautiful young princess and the handsome Frog Prince. The princess grew more and more lovely with the passing of the years and, as was right and proper, the prince grew more and more loving. It is not surprising then that the royal couple lived for ever and ever in joy and happiness!

The Little Match Girl

There was once upon a time a little girl who had no shoes to wear—not even in the winter time. This little girl was perhaps eight years old and she lived in the very poorest part of a big town.

If she had a proper name of her own, no one knew it. She was known everywhere as the little match girl, because each day she went out into the streets to sell bundles of matches.

In the summer the little match girl did not mind that she had no shoes. The sun warmed her bare feet as she went among the shoppers or talked to some of the friends she had made.

There was the pretty young flower-girl who sold tiny bunches of violets to the passing gentlemen, and the street bird-seller with his birds in a large cage. And the watercress girl who always greeted her with a friendly smile.

But in the winter the flower-girl and the watercress girl were no longer to be found, and the little match girl was sure then that she did not have a friend in the world.

Once she did have someone very close to her who had loved her—her grand-mother. But the old lady had died and the match girl had only the memory of her grandmother's love to comfort her.

One year the snows came much earlier than usual. And by Christmas the pavements were slippery with ice, and the cruel wind had whipped the snow into deep drifts against the walls and the shop fronts.

The rich men of the town wore their warmest coats and mufflers and their tall hats to protect them against the biting wind. They were so anxious to be back in their cosy houses that they paid no attention to the little match girl. And they certainly did not think of buying any matches from her.

It is true it was a jolly time of year, but their minds were full of thoughts about the presents they must find for their families, and all the food they would presently be enjoying.

So the little girl sold very few of her bundles of matches over Christmas, and on New Year's Eve her father sent her out again. He was a hard, cruel man with no thought for his child. Even her mother did not pretend to love the little girl, or seem to care that she wore only a thin cotton blouse and patched skirt.

Their attic, its cracks stuffed with straw, was such a miserable place to live that the woman had long ago given up trying to be cheerful or to make those about her happy. She thought only of the money the little girl would give her at the end of the day.

'You can put my old slippers on your feet,' the mother told her daughter, as she gave her the matches. 'And mind you do better than you did yesterday.'

Shivering with cold, the little match girl crept out into the streets. But the slippers were much too big for her small feet, and soon one had fallen off, and a ragged boy snatched it and ran away with it.

Then the other slipper came off and

The rich people of the town were anxious to be back in their cosy houses.

was lost in the snow and the little girl wandered on through the streets, her toes blue with cold.

How she envied the well-dressed ladies of the town with their fur bonnets and fur muffs. How she wished that some of these rich ladies would notice her and out of the kindness of their hearts offer to buy some of her matches.

She waited by the coach and thought sadly that even the old horse had a better coat then she had.

Some of the men carried packages under their arms, for it was still the season of good will and present-giving.

The little match girl had never had a present in her life except a tiny bunch of spring flowers from the flower-girl and that was long ago. And as she stood there hoping she would be noticed, she began to wonder what might be in some of the

69

*They paid no attention to the little match girl
shivering with cold.*

parcels. Perhaps the gentleman in the blue coat was taking a doll home to his granddaughter or a cuddly bear!

She thought she could guess what was in the bottle the big tall man with the red nose was carrying and, as he passed her, she called out hopefully, 'Buy some matches, sir? Please take some!'

But the big tall man did not even turn his head to look her way, and the little girl sighed, wondering whether her father would beat her if she did not make any money that day.

The snow was falling now so thickly that her hair and face were powdered with it, and she was so cold that she could not stop shivering. Yet she dared not go home. If she did, there would be no one to give her a kind word and more than likely her father would turn her out again. And when she thought of home she remembered only the wind whistling through the gaps in the roof and the bare wooden floor and the straw bed upon which she had to lie.

'No, I will not go home,' the little girl told herself bravely. 'Surely some kind lady or gentleman will buy some of my matches before the day is out!'

And she began walking up and down the long street and sometimes approaching one or two of the jollier looking ladies with a shy request that they take home some of her matches.

Sadly, although the ladies and their husbands had only moments before been busy wishing each other happiness for the New Year, they did not think of the girl's happiness or what it would mean to her if they gave her a little money.

When she spoke to them, they looked the other way or buried their faces deep in their high collars or mufflers and hurried on.

Now the little girl was so numb with cold that she felt weak and dizzy and she wandered into the middle of the road and was nearly run down by a horse and carriage. The coachman cracked his whip angrily and shouted, 'Why can't you look where you're going, you stupid little girl!'

And the little match girl was so frightened and startled that she lost some of her precious matches in the snow.

As night approached, the blizzard increased in violence and even the fittest

She was nearly run down by a horse and carriage.

and strongest of the passers-by found it almost impossible to face the biting wind. They huddled inside their heavy over-coats and kept a tight grasp on their umbrellas to stop them from being tugged out of their hands by the cruel blizzard.

'I cannot stay here,' the little girl told herself desperately. 'I must leave the busy streets and find shelter.'

And she dragged her numbed feet away from the crowded pavements and stumbled on towards the quiet part of the big town where the rich people lived.

No one spared her a glance as she wandered away until presently she came to a road which was lined with tall, elegant houses.

How merry the ladies and their friends looked, as they laughed and raised their glasses to each other!

All the houses had lights streaming from their windows, and the little match girl heard the sound of laughter and the tinkling of glass against glass as the people inside toasted each other.

She looked around until she saw a small opening between two of the tall houses which would give her some shelter from the wind, and she went to it and sat down on the steps.

As she crouched there, she could see into one of the windows of the house opposite. How merry the ladies and their friends looked. How they laughed and shouted as they raised their glasses to each other!

And then there came to her the smell of roast goose. It was such a wonderful smell that the little girl closed her eyes in an effort to capture it. She almost forgot how hungry she was as she pictured the fat goose, roasted to a turn, sitting on the table.

There was no thought now in her mind of going home. It was so late that the lamps were all lit in the dark streets, and she had little hope of selling any of her matches. To go home at this hour, without any money, would bring down the anger of both her mother and her father on her head. And she dared not face that! If only her beloved grandmother had been alive —she would have protected her from her parents' anger. She would have drawn her within the shelter of her shawl and cuddled and kissed her and perhaps given her some tiny present which she had managed to make.

The little girl sighed deeply as she pulled the ragged shawl over her head. She would have to stay where she was for the rest of that night. In the morning it

She sat down in a small opening between two houses.

The match began to burn with a warm bright flame.

76

would be the first day of the New Year and perhaps then people would want to buy her matches.

But now her hands were so numb with cold that they had no feeling in them at all. She thought to herself that if only she could draw out one of her matches and rub it against the wall, its flame would warm her fingers.

It was not easy to do this, for her poor fingers were as stiff as boards, but at last she succeeded and she struck the match against the wall.

For an instant it sputtered and seemed to be going out. Then it began to burn with a warm bright flame.

'Why, it is like a Christmas candle!' the little girl thought. And it seemed to her that she was seated in a cosy armchair in front of a warm stove.

The room was small, but there were

She cupped her hand round the bright little flame and stared at the magnificent stove.

heavy curtains on the windows to shut out the cold night air, and there was a pair of woollen slippers, just her size, by the stove.

But the little girl did not think that she had any need of the slippers so long as the stove was there.

It was such a great big stove, all shiny with polish, and it seemed to nod and wink at her as it warmed her feet and her hands and then her cold wet face.

'Oh, how lovely you are!' the little girl whispered. 'How nice of you to warm me. I have never felt so cosy.'

And she cupped her hand round the bright little flame of her match as she stared at the magnificent stove.

Alas, the match burned for just a second longer and then it went out. The big friendly stove vanished, and the little girl found she had only the spent match to look at.

'I must not, I dare not use any more of the matches,' she told herself, as she put the burned-out match on the step beside her. 'But I will not throw this poor match away for it brought me a lovely dream.'

Some hours passed and the little girl began to wonder if she dared strike just one more match.

She was so cold and weak that she knew she would not be able to stand up to do this, but then there was no need.

There was no one to see her wasting her matches, for the gay party in the house on the other side of the street was over. Or perhaps the people had simply drawn the curtains before sitting down to their roast goose.

78

With fingers that were blue with cold the little girl struck another match. It burned up brightly and its light fell upon the wall.

'Oh! How bright you are!' the little girl exclaimed, her eyes fixed upon it.

And then the wall had vanished and

She struck another match, which burned up brightly.

she found she could see into a room. And
there on the table, which was laid with a
snow-white cloth, was a wonderful fat
roasted goose. It sat on a great silver dish
and round it were roast potatoes.

There was stuffing, and two kinds of
sauce, and there were dried sugar plums
and all manner of delicious sweetmeats
on the table besides the bird.

Then, wonder of wonders, the goose
hopped off its silver dish and with a knife
and fork in its beak waddled over to the
little girl and invited her to take one of its
wings.

'That's very kind of you,' the little
girl began to say. 'Yes, please, I would
like that, if you don't mind . . .' when, all

*Wonder of wonders, the goose
hopped off its silver dish.*

at once the match spluttered and went out,
and the goose vanished.

Tears came into the girl's eyes as she
stared at the cold black wall. It had been
such a wonderful sight—that snow-white
table laden with so many good things
to eat!

She knew now that it was not only the bitter weather which was making her feel so weak and helpless. It was also the fact that she had eaten nothing all day long. And without stopping to think she lit her third match.

Once again she found herself looking into a room. It was surely the finest room in the whole world and there in one corner stood the finest tree in the whole world. It was a thousand times more beautiful than any she had ever seen before.

Balls of different colours hung from its branches. And there were candles and shimmering tinsel which sparkled in the light, and from some of the lower branches there hung boxes tied up with pretty silk ribbon. It seemed as though the tree itself was alive.

As she stared at the wonderful tree, a little girl came into the room and she looked just like the match girl except that she was richly dressed in a cape and hood trimmed with fur.

*As she stared at the
wonderful tree, a little girl
came into the room.*

The match girl stretched out her hand to touch the beautiful young stranger, and suddenly the match went out, and the child and the Christmas tree were no longer to be seen.

As soon as her cold stiff fingers would permit, the girl lit another match against the wall and as the flame grew brighter she gave a cry of joy.

There, standing before her, was her own dear grandmother. She was so clear and so close that the little girl reached out to touch her, and the old woman held out her arms and smiled.

'Take me with you! Please take me!' the little girl pleaded. 'I've missed you so much and I want to be with you.'

Her grandmother's wise, gentle face was so kind and inviting that the little girl could not take her eyes away from it. And when her match was nearly ready to burn itself out, she began with frantic haste to strike another.

'Take me with you! Please take me!' the little girl pleaded.

84

*As her grandmother bore
her up to heaven . . .*

86

. . . her days of hunger and want were over for ever.

'Poor child!' he murmured.
'She has frozen to death!'

Each time her match had burned away she had lost something precious. Now at all costs she must keep her grandmother beside her.

But now the old woman was bending over her and gathering her up in her arms, and the little match girl sighed with a deep joy and thankfulness as she felt the warmth and comfort of her grandmother's arms about her. And as her grandmother bore her up to heaven the girl knew that all her days of hunger and want were over for ever.

Early the next morning, on the first day of the New Year, one of the gentlemen from the tall house opposite saw the little girl lying in the snow and he crossed the street to look at her.

'Poor child!' he murmured to himself. 'She has frozen to death. How sad for her!'

Then he saw all the burned matches in the snow and he thought to himself that she had lit them to warm her poor stiff fingers.

But there was something about the little girl which puzzled the old man. It was something about her face. It looked so smiling and peaceful.

'It was almost as if she had seen an angel,' said the old gentleman that night, as he sat cosily sipping wine with his wife by the fire. 'I tell you the child looked quite happy as she lay in the snow.'

'Don't bother your head about her any longer,' said his good wife sharply. 'It is the beginning of the year and there are a great many things to see to.'

And when her husband continued to stare dreamily into the flames and shake his old head, she clattered the fire-tongs noisily. 'There now!' she went on, annoyed that her husband was not paying her the attention she thought she deserved. 'Who cares about a match girl? The town is full of them and if I had my way I'd see to it that they were all kept at home in such terrible, wintry weather . . .'

'It may be,' said her husband mildly, 'that the child had nowhere to go. What on earth could have brought that smile to her face—it was such a happy one?'

And the old gentleman would continue to wonder—for how could he possibly guess that the little match girl had been smiling at someone as beautiful as her grandmother?

Donkey-Skin

Once upon a time there was a powerful king who had everything in the world a king could possibly desire. His palace was filled with priceless furniture and works of art. His gardens bloomed with the most beautiful and rare flowers and bushes. And in his magnificent stables were stallions and mares which were the envy of all other kings and emperors.

Strange to relate, there was also a little donkey in the stables. It was just a very ordinary little donkey with big eyes and big ears, but for some reason which the king would not explain it had won his respect and admiration. Indeed, many of the king's ministers believed the king cherished the little donkey above all his other grand possessions.

This powerful king had a very lovely wife and a daughter who was so like her beautiful mother in appearance that when the two went out walking together they were often taken for sisters.

One day the king's happiness was shattered by the sudden illness of his dear wife. She was so many years younger than himself that the idea that she might die before him came as a great shock.

He summoned to her bedside all the finest doctors in the land who tried their skills to save her. But the mysterious illness quite baffled them.

'We cannot save her,' they told the king at last. 'There is nothing we can do. Your lady wife will die before the sun rises on another day.'

'I am the most powerful king in the whole world,' the old man cried. 'It is my command that you save her!'

But the doctors shook their heads and muttered into their beards or stroked their chins, and the king knew that they could do nothing to save his wife.

Then he hurried to her bedside and begged her to live for his sake. The young queen smiled sadly at his words.

'I know I am about to die,' she said gently. 'Will you promise me just one thing and I shall die happily?'

'Anything, anything,' murmured the king. 'You know you have only to ask.'

'When I am gone,' said the queen, 'I want you to marry again.'

'Never, never!' cried the king.

'It is my wish,' said the queen in a firm voice. 'But it is also my wish that you choose a wife who is even more beautiful than I, and who is wiser. Promise that you will do this . . .'

The poor king bowed his head and wept at his wife's words, but he gave his solemn promise and the queen gave a happy sigh and closed her eyes. Within the hour she had gone to heaven.

The king summoned to her bedside all the finest doctors in the land.

A strange madness then took possession of the sorrowing king. For days he did not speak and when at last he opened his mouth, it appeared to those who were close to him that he had lost his senses.

He began talking as if he were once again a young man. He talked about himself as the prince, saying over and over again that he must find a beautiful young princess and make her his wife.

He seemed a hundred years old as he sat there in his chair with his eyes closed, but at other time he was wide awake and talked of matters which would interest only a young man.

The physicians who had come to take care of the queen now stayed on to look after the king. They feared that soon he would be truly mad and not fit to rule his vast country.

And when the young princess begged to be allowed to see her father, the doctors shook their heads, saying that he would not know who she was.

Well, this sad, sad state of affairs went on for a month or more and it seemed to all those who knew the king that he was in the grip of some strange madness which could not be cured.

One day, while walking in the gardens, the mad old king caught sight of the lovely princess in the distance.

'There she is!' he cried. 'There is the girl I will marry.'

'But sire,' one of his attendants said. 'That is the princess, your daughter, you see over there by the fountain.'

He sat in his chair with his eyes closed.

'There is the girl I will marry,' cried the king.

'No, no, I tell you she is a stranger to me—and yet—and yet I have lost my poor heart to her.'

That night he told one of the courtiers to bring the lovely princess to him, and the horrified girl, who adored her father, was greatly saddened when she heard him speak of himself as her future husband. But she had been warned to say nothing that would upset or disturb him, and so she remained silent as the old man began to speak of marriage.

Now the princess had a wonderful godmother, who was in fact a fairy, and the next day she went to see her.

'I know why you have come,' the fairy godmother said, as soon as the princess entered her room. 'You are worried about your father, the king.'

'Yes, yes,' cried the princess, kneeling at the feet of the wise old woman. 'Tell me what to do? My poor father is unwell.'

'Whatever you do,' said her godmother, 'must be done with the greatest kindness. You must not hurt or distress your father at this time. Trust me and follow my advice and all will turn out well.'

'Tell me what I must do then?' said the princess. 'What do I say when next he asks me to marry him?'

'You must say nothing to that. Instead ask him for a present. Say that you must have a dress the colour of the sky. He will not be able to grant such a request for the sky has many colours, and then you will be free to tell him the truth.'

The princess was encouraged by her godmother's advice, for she knew how wise and good she was and she returned to the palace full of hope.

The princess knelt at the feet of the wise old woman.

That night when the king sent for her and she stood, trembling, in his presence, she kept silent as he began making plans for the wedding. Then she cried, 'But first, sire, I must have a dress the colour of the sky.'

'The colour of the sky!' exclaimed the old king. 'And why not?' And as the girl left the room he called for the royal tailors and told them that they must find material the colour of the sky and make from it a dress for the princess.

'I want the dress by tomorrow,' he said. 'If you fail me in this matter, you will all be executed!'

With such a terrible fate hanging over their heads, the tailors set about their task with all speed. They found an aged dressmaker who was so clever with her needle that she could embroider the moon and stars on the blue satin they brought her. And when her embroidery was completed, they cut out the wonderful material and worked on it right through the night.

Even so, the dress was not finished when the old king asked for it to be shown to the princess.

'It will take but an hour or two more to complete it, Your Majesty,' said one of

The weavers worked on the material all night.

the tailors. 'The princess shall have her dress by the afternoon.'

The princess hid her dismay as well as she could when she heard this. And she left the palace and made her way to her fairy godmother's house.

'What shall I do?' she wailed, as soon as she saw her godmother.

'You must ask him for a dress as bright

The princess hid her dismay as well as she could.

and shining as the sun,' the fairy told her. 'He will never be able to grant you such a request and then you will be free.'

But the old king, when the princess informed him that she must have such a dress, sent for his best jewelers. After warning them that they would lose their heads if they failed him, he told them they must procure such a dress.

They made a dress out of gold cloth and trimmed it with diamonds. When the dress was finished, it was so dazzling that the princess could scarcely look at it. But it was also so beautiful that she longed to wear it right away! Instead she went to her godmother to tell her that once again the king had managed to grant her request.

'Please tell me what to do now?' she begged tearfully. 'I have the dress that looks like the sky and the dress that looks

*The dress was so
dazzling that the
princess could
scarcely look at it.*

like the sun. Is there anything I can ask my
father which he will not give me?'

'Is there anything he sets great store
upon?' asked the fairy.

'Why, yes, the little donkey that he
keeps in the stables,' cried the princess.
'You know how he loves the animal!'

'I know,' said the fairy godmother,
'And though it will be hard for you—you
must ask him for the donkey's skin!'

'He will never, never grant me that

request,' declared the princess, her tears forgotten. 'I will ask him.'

Early next morning the princess asked the king for the donkey's skin. 'Nothing else will do,' she said, thinking that her father would refuse.

To her surprise and horror the king gave orders that his donkey should be destroyed and its skin brought to her.

His face was so lined with sorrow and grief as he gave the order that the princess ran from his presence so that he would not see her own tears.

And when the donkey's skin was laid at her feet that same day, she wept as if her heart would break.

That night her fairy godmother came

The king gave orders that his donkey should be destroyed.

The fairy packed the small chest and gave her a magic wand.

to her and told her that she must leave the palace.

'You must go disguised as a servant,' she said. 'Wear the donkey's skin. It will hide your beauty.'

Then the fairy packed a small chest with the princess's beautiful gowns and her jewels. To these she added a mirror and all the necessary things the princess would need while she was so far from home. Then she said, 'Take my magic wand. When you wish to have the chest you have only to wave the wand and it will appear.'

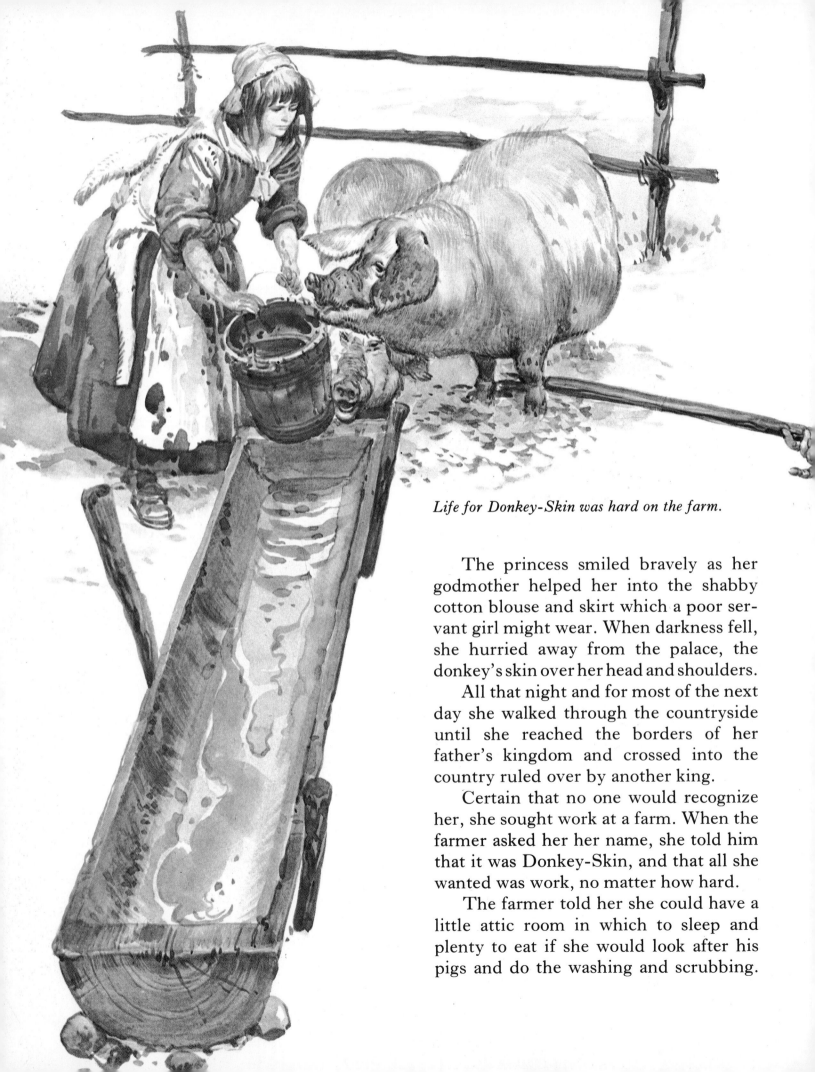

Life for Donkey-Skin was hard on the farm.

The princess smiled bravely as her godmother helped her into the shabby cotton blouse and skirt which a poor servant girl might wear. When darkness fell, she hurried away from the palace, the donkey's skin over her head and shoulders.

All that night and for most of the next day she walked through the countryside until she reached the borders of her father's kingdom and crossed into the country ruled over by another king.

Certain that no one would recognize her, she sought work at a farm. When the farmer asked her her name, she told him that it was Donkey-Skin, and that all she wanted was work, no matter how hard.

The farmer told her she could have a little attic room in which to sleep and plenty to eat if she would look after his pigs and do the washing and scrubbing.

'I will do anything you say,' said Donkey-Skin gratefully. And she followed him to the pig sty where he showed her the pigs which would be in her charge.

Life for Donkey-Skin was hard on the farm. The work itself was very unpleasant and the lads teased her because she looked so plain and ugly in her big donkey's skin.

'Don't know why you stay!' one of the ragged little boys, who haunted the place, said one day. 'But then you look so awful no one will ever give you a proper position. Certainly not our master, who is a friend of the young prince! He likes pretty girls about the house.'

The princess longed to tell the cheeky young boy who she really was, but wisely she held her tongue. No one must ever guess that she was anything but Donkey-Skin, a poor serving girl.

The lads teased her because she looked so plain in her big donkey's skin.

The young prince had a passion for beautiful, exotic birds.

One day the young prince came to the farm to see some of the beautiful, exotic birds which the farmer kept.

These birds, many of them from sunny islands across the seas, had long been a passion with the king's son, and whenever he could escape from his palace, he came to the aviary to admire them.

Donkey-Skin had seen the young man at a distance and it seemed to her that he had a kind, gentle face. She, too, was fond

of the birds and it pleased her to watch him in secret as he wandered among them.

That night, after the farmer and all the servants had gone to bed, she took her fairy godmother's magic wand and waved it. Immediately the chest appeared and she went to it eagerly and opened it. Inside were all her most lovely dresses, and after washing her face with the rare perfumed soap that was also in the chest, and combing her long golden hair with her silver comb, she put on one of her dresses and walked up and down the tiny room as if she were at home.

It was so lovely to be a princess again! The fairy had known that sooner or later she would want to dress up! And then she thought of the handsome prince and wished that he could see her now!

'But that must not be,' the princess sighed. 'I am Donkey-Skin in his eyes and must remain so.'

The following Sunday, which was a day of rest for Donkey-Skin, the king's son visited the aviary once again. And after wandering for some time among his feathered friends, he sat down on a log below the girl's window.

She peeped down on him from behind the curtain and was lost in admiration as he made friends with one of the fiercer birds which the farmer used for falconry.

He made friends with one of the fiercer birds used for falconry.

'How patient he is,' she thought. 'How delightfully his brown hair curls!' And she longed to call out to him.

But the prince did not look up and after a time he wearied of his pastime and got up and strode away.

As he was about to mount his horse and ride away, the farmer saw him and invited him to stay to a meal.

'You are very welcome to make yourself at home,' said the farmer, who was not much older than the prince. 'Stay a while and we can discuss some of the plans I have made to enlarge the aviary.'

'I will be glad to,' said the prince. And he tethered his horse and followed his host into the farmhouse.

While the farmer went off into the servants' quarters to warn them of his royal guest, the prince wandered off down one of the long passages. The farm was old and the building interested him. Presently he came to some narrow stairs at the back of the house and, curious as to where they led, he climbed them and soon found himself at the top of the ancient building.

There were several small rooms which opened out on to the landing, and the prince, with a slight, mischievous smile, put his eye to one of the keyholes and peered inside.

Now it happened that the princess, knowing that she would be left to herself for the rest of the day, had taken out her magic wand. Using it, she had summoned the chest and to amuse herself she had taken out one of the beautiful dresses and put it on.

The hateful donkey's skin lay on the floor at her feet while she busied herself with her toilet.

Through his spy-hole the young man saw a girl so wonderful that he felt stunned by her beauty.

Her hair was golden in the light which streamed through the attic window; her skin was white and soft, and round her slender neck was a collar of sparkling diamonds.

'I must speak with her,' he told himself as he struggled to his feet. 'I must find out who she is.'

And he put out his hand to knock at the door which stood between him and the vision of beauty.

Once, twice, three times he tried to force himself to knock. But the fear that the girl would reproach him for spying upon her always swept over him and held him back. And at last the prince crept away from the door and down the stairs.

The farmer reproached him gently for going off by himself and the prince smiled and said nothing of what he had seen.

Instead, as they sat down to a meal, he asked if there were many young girls with golden hair working on the farm.

'Never a one!' laughed the farmer. 'The only maid we have who works outside for the most part is Donkey-Skin. Oh, she's a nice enough girl I suppose, and she does her work well—but you would hardly call her pretty.'

The prince asked no further questions, but he returned to his palace in a very thoughtful mood. No matter how hard he tried, he could not forget the lovely girl he had seen.

A week passed and the young man was so pale and restless that his mother, the queen, feared he might be ill.

'Ride over to the farm,' she suggested. 'You know how much you enjoy looking

at the pretty birds. Perhaps your friend will ask you to stay for a while.'

The prince set off almost at once, and as soon as he had left his horse with a stable boy, went on foot to the aviary.

There—to his delight—was the girl he had spied upon. As she stood, framed in the open window, she was like a picture—a painting so rare and lovely that the young man could only stare up at her at a loss for words.

But no sooner did the princess realize

As she stood, framed in the open window, she was like a picture.

'Don't joke with me, young sir,' said the poultry woman.

she was being watched than she hurriedly shut the window and disappeared inside her room, leaving the young man in such a state that he felt he was unable to meet his friend. Instead he sought out the old poultry woman whom he had known some years.

'Tell me,' said he, 'about the girl who lives here. She is—well as lovely as the sun itself—and richly attired as if she were some kind of princess.'

'Do not joke with me, young sir,' said the old woman. 'You can't mean Donkey-

Skin and there is no other young girl on the farm.'

'I tell you I saw her,' the prince burst out, growing red and pale by turns. 'She must be here . . .'

And when the old woman only laughed and shrugged her shoulders the prince mounted his horse and galloped home.

That night he refused all food and was so clearly in the grip of some sickness that his anxious parents sent for their two royal physicians.

The doctors discussed the prince's sad condition in whispers as he lay, without movement, in the bed prepared for him. But they could offer no suggestions for a cure, and the distraught king and queen knelt by their son's bedside in the vain hope that he would open his eyes and speak to them.

'You must fight against this dreadful illness which has struck you down,' the queen urged her son, as she bent over him. 'Try to tell us how we may help you. Is there anything you want? Someone, perhaps, you may wish to see?'

At this the young prince opened his eyes briefly and murmured weakly, 'I want Donkey-Skin! Donkey-Skin must come . . .' before once again drifting away into a state of unconsciousness.

'Donkey-Skin? Who or what is Donkey-Skin?' the king demanded, as he followed his wife out of the sick-room.

'I have no idea,' said the queen, 'but we must find out immediately.'

Their astonishment was great when one of the servants informed them that Donkey-Skin was one of the servants who worked at the farm. 'And the scruffiest

The doctors could offer no suggestions for a cure.

little tramp of a girl you ever set eyes on, Your Majesty,' the servant added, as the king rewarded him for coming forward.

'I don't understand,' the queen said in a low voice to her husband. 'Perhaps we misheard what our son was saying.'

But the next day when they returned to the prince's bedside, he opened his eyes for a moment and once again murmured the same name adding in a feeble whisper, 'She must bake a cake for me!'

So by royal command Donkey-Skin was given the freedom of the farmer's kitchen, and, because her task was such an important one, she washed her face and combed her hair and wore a pretty dress,

She made the cake when there was no one about.

and the tiny gold ring with an emerald stone which her fairy godmother had once given her.

She made the cake during the night when there was no one about, but as she mixed the dough, the tiny gold ring slipped off her finger into the mixture.

Early the next morning the cake was delivered to the prince and to everyone's joyful surprise he asked for a slice and seemed to be marvellously better on eating

The king's proclamation was read in every village, town and city.

it. But as he took a bite of the second piece he nearly swallowed the band of gold. To the king's amazement he declared that his illness could only be completely cured if he married the girl who could wear the tiny gold and emerald ring.

'Yes, yes, of course,' said the king, wishing only to please his son. 'I will send out a proclamation at once. All the girls in our kingdom will be given the chance to try on this ring.'

The king's proclamation was read in every village, town and city, and soon

girls came flocking to the palace to try
their luck.

There came first beautiful princesses
and duchesses whose hands were soft and
white but whose fingers were much too
plump for the slender band of gold.

Then came the turn of the serving
girls, and you may be sure they tried as
eagerly as the high-born ladies to force
the ring on to their fingers.

At last it was Donkey-Skin's turn and
the tiny band of gold slipped over her

*The tiny band of
gold slipped over
her slender finger.*

slender finger so easily that those watching sent up a shout of amazement.

'Before I am presented to the prince,' said she, 'let me go back to the farm to make myself respectable.'

Once there she put on her shimmering sun dress and returned to the palace where the royal party awaited her.

'Is she not beautiful?' cried the happy prince, now quite cured of his illness.

'Beautiful indeed!' agreed the queen. 'We shall arrange the marriage quickly.'

Never had there been such a wedding, for it was attended by all the emperors, the kings and rajahs in the world. But the most important guest was the princess's own father whose madness left him the moment he saw her dressed as a bride.

So Donkey-Skin, as the prince sometimes teasingly called her, was now completely happy and remained so for the rest of her days!

'Is she not beautiful?' cried the happy prince.

The Good Fairy

There was once upon a time a good fairy who set great store on politeness. She knew, of course, that most sensible people are polite to fairies, so she went about in disguise. Sometimes she would appear as a poor peasant woman, sometimes as a rich countess. Then if the person she met passed her test, she would grant them a special favour.

One day the good fairy, having nothing much to do, left her kingdom to look for a worthy child for her favours. And there, by a spring in the forest, she saw a young girl in a shabby red and white dress.

The girl's face, framed by a mass of golden hair, was so gentle and pretty that the fairy made up her mind to put her to the test and she approached her in the guise of a poor peasant woman.

'Will you give a thirsty old woman a drink from your pitcher?' she asked.

'Gladly, mother,' smiled the girl. 'But first let me make certain the water is fit for drinking.' And she emptied and then carefully rinsed the pitcher before filling it from the spring.

'I am surprised that you go to so much trouble for a stranger,' the fairy said, after she had sipped the water.

'It is nothing,' the pretty girl said politely. 'Drink as much as you want. It will be no bother to fill the pitcher again.

Only I must do it quickly or else my step-mother will beat me for staying too long at the spring.'

'Does she often beat you?' asked the fairy.

'Yes,' the girl admitted. 'For some reason she hates the sight of me. I can't seem to do anything right especially when it is for Fanchon . . .'

'Fanchon?'

'Fanchon is my stepsister. She and her mother are awfully like each other,' the girl confessed. 'I mean they have the same long noses and fierce tempers . . .'

'Dear me!' exclaimed the fairy, hiding a smile. 'It can't be easy to live with such an unpleasant pair. Well, I can see you are unhappy but you can still manage to be kind and polite to a stranger.' She paused and then she continued, 'I have decided to grant you a favour.'

The girl looked at her in surprise. 'There is no need,' she began, but the good fairy cut her short. 'When you get home,' she said, 'I declare that a flower or a precious stone will fall from your mouth with every word you utter . . .'

And, as was her custom after she had granted one of her favours, she vanished into the forest.

After she had filled her pitcher with water for the second time, the girl set out

for home. She had barely time to enter the kitchen before her stepmother was raging at her for taking so long.

As she opened her mouth to tell of her meeting with the peasant woman, three rubies, four diamonds and two pearls fell from her lips, and soon the table was covered with precious stones and flowers.

'Well, it must have been a fairy,' said her stepmother when she had heard the full story. 'If only it had been my own dear Fanchon! But it is not too late. Fanchon will go to the spring this very day and no doubt the fairy will come to her in the same disguise.'

Then she went to her cupboard and brought out a silver pitcher, thinking that the fairy would be even more liberal with her favours if she had a drink from such a fine flagon.

But when Fanchon heard that she must go to the spring, she began to protest.

By a spring in the forest, she saw a young girl in a shabby red and white dress.

*The grand lady asked Fanchon to fill
her pitcher and allow her to drink from it.*

'I'm not accustomed to walk such a
long way,' she whined. 'And anyway why
should I go to all that trouble?'

'You'll do as you are told,' her fierce
mother screamed at her. 'Here take this
pitcher and remember your manners
when the old peasant woman addresses
you.'

And when she still hesitated, her long-
nosed mother pushed her out of the house
shouting, 'Hurry along now and don't
drop my silver pitcher.'

Grumbling to herself at having to walk
so far, Fanchon arrived at the spring in a
very bad temper, but remembering her
mother's warning she made up her mind
to be as nice as possible when the fairy-
woman appeared. She was wondering if
she should take off her high-heeled shoes
to rest her feet when she saw a tall lady,
elegantly dressed, coming towards her
out of the forest.

The grand lady asked Fanchon if she
would fill her pitcher from the spring and
allow her to drink from it.

'What!' Fanchon cried. 'You ask me to
do the work of a servant? Do you think I
carried my pitcher all the way here just to
let you drink from it? What do you take
me for?'

'You are not very polite,' said the
stranger, without any sign of anger, for
fairies, especially good ones, know how to
hide their feelings. 'But I hope you will
agree that one bad turn deserves another.
For your rudeness I declare that with
every word you utter a snake or a toad will
fall from your mouth!'

Fanchon tossed her head to show that
she did not believe a word of this and
before she could say as much the lady was
no longer there.

Out came toads and snakes.

'She certainly wasn't the fairy-woman,' the girl thought. 'She was a countess or a duchess! I'll wait on.'

But though she waited an hour or more, the peasant woman did not appear and so, in a very bad temper, she made her way home.

Her mother was watching out for her and though she was bursting with eagerness to lay her hands on all the diamonds, pearls and rubies which she knew would presently fall from her daughter's mouth, she would not allow Fanchon to say a word until she had conducted her into the drawing-room. There they would be safe from prying eyes.

Still with her finger to her lips she motioned Fanchon to a comfortable chair before crying, 'Speak, daughter, speak!'

Alas, when Fanchon opened her mouth, out came three toads and two snakes!

'Your stepsister is responsible for this!' the furious woman screamed. 'I'll teach her a lesson she won't forget!'

And she grabbed a stick and beat her stepdaughter before driving her out of the house and into the forest. As the poor girl sat weeping bitterly at her miserable lot, a king's son happened to ride by. Moved by her tears, he asked her why she was so sad.

The girl told him her story and, with every word, diamonds and rubies fell from her lips. Charmed by her gentle manner and—even more—by the fortune that lay at her feet, the prince, there and then, asked her to marry him, and she agreed at once!

So the fairy's good deed for that day was well and truly done. As for the unkind stepsister and her mother, they had to share their house with nasty toads and snakes for the rest of their lives!

A king's son happened to ride by.

Red Riding Hood

Once upon a time there was a little girl who lived with her father and mother in a cottage on the edge of a big dark wood.

Everybody loved the dear little girl, and she was especially loved by her kind old Grandmamma who lived on the other side of the big wood in a cottage of her own.

When her Grandmamma was younger and was able to see well enough to make tiny neat stitches, she had sat down and cut out and sewn a beautiful cape and hood for her granddaughter. It was made out of a rich red velvet and it looked very handsome and cosy when it was finished.

The little girl could scarcely wait to try on the lovely cape and hood when it arrived. And when her mother had helped her to fasten it round her neck and tucked her ribbons under the hood, she had danced all round the kitchen in it.

From the moment of its arrival the little girl wore her red cape and hood as often as her mother would allow. She wore it about the house and in the garden, and she wore it to go to the village shops.

'Why, hello, little Red Riding Hood,' smiled the baker, when he saw her in it for the first time, and he gave her a biscuit covered with sticky sugar.

'Good-day to you, Red Riding Hood,' said the lady who sold sweets, when she saw her for the first time in her new outfit. And she gave her a handful of toffees.

'That's a fine bright red you're in today,' said the jolly fishmonger. And he gave her a little fish for her pussy cat who was waiting at home for her, before adding, 'You're a proper little Red Riding Hood you are!'

Soon everybody in the village was calling the little girl Red Riding Hood and if she had another name, which I'm sure she did, it was forgotten. Even her mother and her father called their golden-haired daughter Red Riding Hood.

Now although Red Riding Hood was old enough to go to the village shops all by herself and to help Mummy with all the dusting and the baking, she was not old enough to go into the dark woods.

This was mostly because of the big bad wolf who lived there. There were all kinds of scary stories about the big bad wolf which the boys in the village told each other in the evenings. And the very boldest of them would boast that they had seen the dreadful wolf among the trees as they walked in the woods.

Little Red Riding Hood knew about the fierce wolf, but she did not think about him much. She was such a gay, happy little girl that she found it hard to believe in witches or ogres or big bad wolves!

One morning, when Red Riding Hood was out in the garden pretending to chase the pretty butterflies, one of the huntsmen, a friend of her father's, came to the house. He had a message from Grandmamma. She had caught a very bad cold and was ill in bed and unable to do her shopping.

'Dear, oh, dear!' exclaimed little Red Riding Hood's mother. And she called her daughter in from the garden.

'Grandmamma is ill,' she told her. 'And I've promised to go into the village and help Mrs Brown today.'

'If you put some nice things in your shopping basket, I could take them to my Grandmamma,' said Red Riding Hood.

'That's a good idea,' said her mother with a sigh of relief. 'Now go and play in the garden again while I get the basket ready for you to take.'

So Red Riding Hood ran back into the garden and began her game again. But now there wasn't any fun in pretending to chase the butterflies. All she could think about was her poor Grandmamma lying ill in bed and perhaps needing her.

While little Red Riding Hood was in the garden, her mother took some delicious sugary doughnuts out of her tin and wrapped them up in some paper. Then she looked out a pot of honey and some fresh cream and a loaf of freshly baked bread and a slab of country butter.

There were so many things she found to put in the basket that she began to wonder whether little Red Riding Hood would be able to carry it.

When she was satisfied at last that she had packed the basket with everything Grandmamma might want, she covered its contents with a white cloth and called her daughter in from the garden.

While little Red Riding Hood was in the garden, her mother filled a basket with delicious food.

'Now remember,' she said, 'don't tip up the basket.'

'I'll remember,' the little girl said, as she put on her beautiful red cape. 'I'll hold it ever so carefully.'

'And give my fond love to Grandmamma,' went on her mother as she walked with Red Riding Hood to the door. 'And tell her I'll be over tomorrow.'

'Yes, I'll do that,' Red Riding Hood said, taking the basket as they got outside.

'One thing more,' said her mother. 'Take the long way round. On no account must you go through the woods.'

'Of course not,' said the little girl.

She promised her mother that she would not go through the woods.

And away she went, taking the long dusty road that went all round the woods and ended up at her Grandmamma's cottage. What a lovely day it was! And oh how inviting the woods were with all the pretty flowers peeping through!

Once or twice Red Riding Hood found her feet taking her off the dusty old road and on to the grass.

It was so beautiful in the woods and such fun to be following the narrow woodland paths.

'It would save time,' she began to think. 'It would save lots of time if I took one of the short cuts through the woods. I wonder if I should?'

And before you could say Jack Robin, there she was, off the road, and into the pretty woods.

It was so beautiful in the woods, and such fun to be following the narrow woodland paths that Red Riding Hood did not give that big bad wolf a single thought. In fact she forgot all about him!

But he was there all right—and he was watching her! He licked his lips as he saw the little girl put down her basket and begin gathering some of the pretty flowers all about her. And at the sight of his fierce greedy look the scared little rabbits fled away to their burrows thankful that just for once the bad old wolf was not interested in them.

As for Red Riding Hood—well, she was thinking how the flowers would please her Grandmamma. So you can imagine what a surprise she got when the wolf at last made up his mind to show himself!

'Well, well, well,' said he, putting on a very mild and tame expression. 'What a pleasure to come across such a sweet child in the woods! Where are you going, my pretty? You can tell old wolfie.'

The wolf's voice was so friendly that Red Riding Hood, after her first start of fear, turned to him with a smile, 'I'm on my way to Grandmamma's cottage on the far side of these woods,' she said. 'These flowers are for her.'

'What a lucky old lady she must be,'

'I'm on my way to Grandmamma's cottage,' she said. 'These flowers are for her.'

said the wolf. 'Lives all alone, does she? On the other side of the wood you said? I must say I'd like somebody as pretty as you to visit me.'

'I've got all sorts of nice things in my basket for her,' said Red Riding Hood. 'I know she will be pleased to see me for she is not very well today.'

'Well, I won't delay you,' said the wolf. 'Goodbye my dear.'

And the wolf disappeared with a bound through the trees, leaving Red Riding Hood to finish gathering her flowers. If he was going to get to that cottage before her he would have to hurry.

Well, that big bad wolf was quite out of breath when Grandmamma's cottage

The wolf disappeared,
leaving Red Riding Hood
to finish gathering her
flowers.

came in sight, and he sat down for a moment to rest before going up to the door.

'Who is it?' came the old lady's feeble voice in answer to his knock.

'It's your own little Red Riding Hood,' replied the wolf. 'I have a lovely basket full of good things to eat.'

'I can't get up,' called out the old lady. 'Lift the latch and come in.'

The wolf lifted the latch. The door opened, and he was inside. Surely if he hadn't been such a dreadfully wicked old wolf the sight of the sweet little lady would have melted his heart. But he *was* a dreadfully wicked old wolf and so he ran to the bed and swallowed little Red Riding Hood's Grandmamma in one gulp.

Then he jumped into bed, put on her frilly white nightcap, tying its pink ribbon in a bow under his chin, and lay back comfortably to wait.

'I shall pretend to be the old lady,' the cunning wolf told himself. The child will be easily deceived. Pity she is so small— but she'll make a tasty morsel.'

The wolf lifted the latch of the door.

'Who is it?' came the old lady's feeble voice in answer to his knock.

131

In the meantime Red Riding Hood was drawing near to the cottage and she ran up the path and knocked at the door just as the wolf had done.

'Who is it?' the wolf called out.

'It's your very own little Red Riding Hood,' came the reply.

'Lift the latch, child,' the wolf said, 'and come straight in!' And he pulled down the white nightcap as far as it would go hoping to hide his ears, and he tightened the pink ribbon to hold it in place. Then he slipped under the bed-clothes so that they would hide his long whiskers and his cruel white teeth.

'I'm coming, Grandmamma,' the little girl shouted excitedly and, as the door sprang open, she skipped into the room.

'Come closer, come closer,' the wolf said in a hoarse whisper, as Red Riding Hood stood at the foot of the bed. 'Come closer and speak to your old Granny.'

'But—but Grandmamma,' said the girl, thinking her Grandmamma looked very, very strange. 'What big ears you have!'

'All the better to hear you with, my child,' came the reply.

'But Grandmamma, what big eyes you have!' said little Red Riding Hood.

'All the better to see you with, my dear!'

'But Grandmamma, what great big hands you have!' cried the little girl.

'All the better to hug you with,' came the reply.

And then, just for a moment, the wolf lifted his head and Red Riding Hood caught sight of his huge mouth and she called out, half in fear and half in surprise, 'Oh, Grandmamma, what a terrible big mouth you have!'

Now by this time the old wolf was in no doubt what he was going to do. He was going to leap out of bed and swallow the little girl in one gulp.

'Come closer child, do,' he said in a croaky whisper. 'Your old Granny wants to smell those pretty flowers you have picked in the woods.'

'You don't seem like my Grandmamma,' whispered Red Riding Hood. And instead of going up to the bed she turned away and put her basket down on the table.

The old wolf fumed with impatience as he said, 'Come, child, come closer.'

'But, Grandmamma,' the little girl said

'Come closer, come closer,' said the wolf.

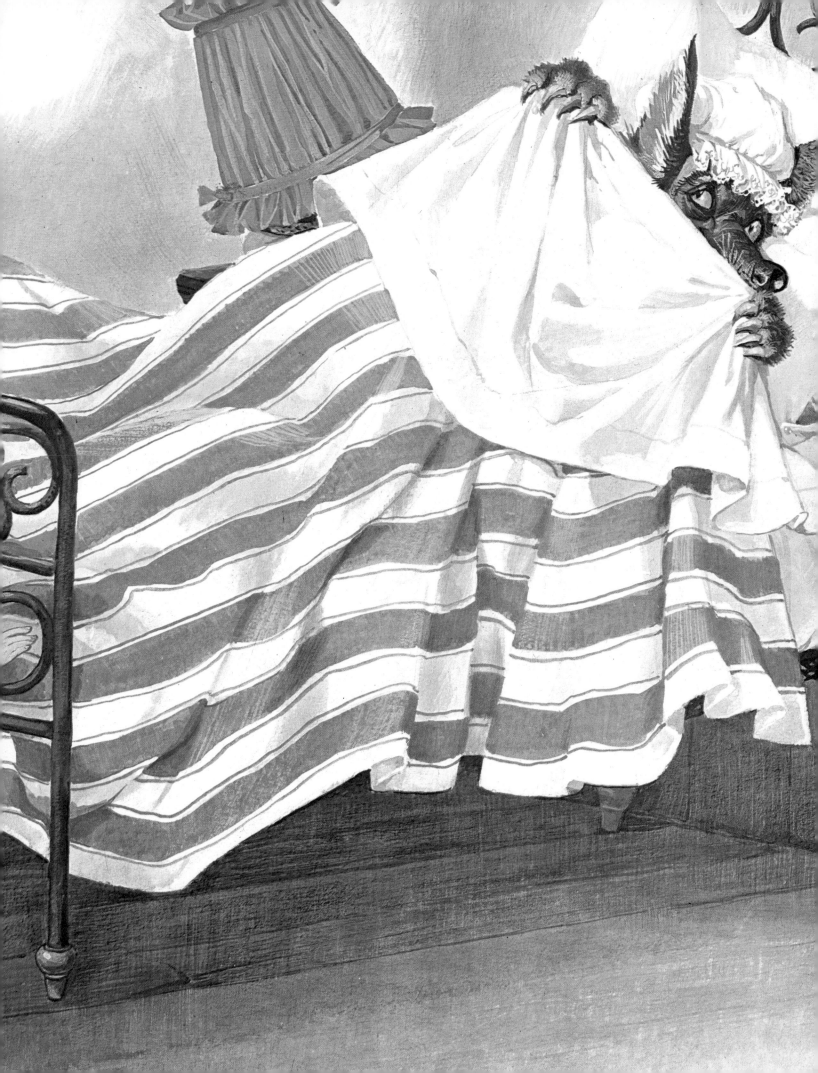

'But—but Grandmamma,
what big ears you have!

in a whisper, 'You are so strange today
and you have such a terrible big mouth!'

'Oh-ho—all the better to eat you
with!' howled the wolf, as the little girl at
last came closer. And with a single bound
he leapt out of bed and there and then
gobbled her up.

Now that wicked, greedy old wolf had
had Grandmamma and little Red Riding
Hood for his dinner, so it was no wonder
that he began to feel very sleepy. He jumped back into bed, put his head on the pillow
and was soon fast asleep and snoring.

With a single bound he leapt out of bed.

His loud snores attracted the attention of a passing huntsman. 'Why the old lady must be ill if she is snoring so loudly, I'll just take a peep through her window to see if she is all right.'

His loud snores
attracted the attention
of a huntsman who was
passing that way.

He raised his gun and shot the wolf dead.

Well, it didn't take him long to work out what had happened when he saw the old wolf. Raising his gun, he aimed at the wicked creature through the window, and shot him dead.

Then the huntsman, sad and sorry that he had arrived too late to save the old lady, put the wolf on the table and took out his big hunting scissors, thinking that he would have the wolf's skin.

Imagine his delighted surprise when,

with the very first snip—out popped the old lady! And with his second snip—out came little Red Riding Hood!

'That was kind of you,' said little Red Riding Hood's Grandmamma. 'I didn't enjoy being inside that horrid creature a bit.'

'Nor me!' said little Red Riding Hood, and she reached up and gave the brave huntsman a big kiss.

Soon all three were sitting down to a

lovely tea of bread and honey and the sweet, sugary doughnuts which Red Riding Hood's mother had put in the basket. And after tea Grandmamma declared that she felt well enough to take care of herself for the rest of the day. So the huntsman and Red Riding Hood went off together through the woods, and there was no big bad wolf to scare the little girl on the way home!

Out popped the old lady and little Red Riding Hood!

Mother Holle

There was once a rich young widow who had two daughters, Erica and Greta. Erica was like her mother in every way. She had a quick temper and a proud manner, and though she was not exactly ugly she was by no means pretty.

Greta, on the other hand, was sweet and gentle and had such a kind heart that she would weep if by chance she stepped on a beetle and killed it. She had also the good fortune to be extremely lively and pretty and greatly admired by her mother's friends and neighbours.

Now you might think that the widow would favour Greta, her youngest. But this was not so. Erica was her favourite and she showed this in a hundred different ways as the two girls grew up.

It was Erica who had the best room in the house and all the smartest dresses she wanted. And it was Erica who was allowed to spend her days in idleness while her sister did all the housework.

Greta was no better than a servant to her mother and sister, and though she worked hard and did not complain, she failed to win a single word of love or encouragement from her hard-hearted mother.

As sometimes happens, Erica treated her young sister as harshly as her mother, for there was no one to correct her or tell her how to behave. Everything she said and did found favour with her mother. She grew up selfish, proud, lazy and disagreeable, and with no friends at all.

The house in which they lived was large, for the widow, though still young, had had two husbands and both, on their deaths, had left her their fortunes. But she could see no reason to employ servants when she had Greta to order about!

It was Greta do this! Greta do that! all day long, and as both the widow and Erica were great bullies at heart, they liked to show off their power and make unreasonable demands on poor Greta.

It was Greta who had to make the beds and dust the rooms. It was Greta who had to wash and polish the floors, and if by chance she finished all her work by the afternoon, she was put to spinning.

Greta worked so hard that she had little time to be sorry for herself, but sometimes, when she found herself alone in the bare, miserable attic which served as her bedroom, she would ask herself why her mother and sister were so cruel to her.

'I do everything they ask of me,' she told herself one night, 'and yet they are not satisfied. Why should Erica have all the pretty dresses when she does nothing? Why do they always look upon me as their poor servant?'

It was Greta who had to wash and polish the floors.

Well, there was no one to answer Greta's questions and no one to comfort her, and the next morning when she went downstairs, she found the kitchen floor covered all over with mud.

'You're late!' snapped her mother.

'She's growing lazy in her old age,' Erica giggled. 'Tell her to get on with the scrubbing, Mother!'

Greta sighed as she filled the bucket and got down on her knees to wash the big stone floor. The work was made all the harder by her mother's and sister's presence, for both took pleasure in pointing out all the places she had missed.

Poor Greta was ready to cry by the time she had finished. But that was only

the beginning of the unhappiest day in her life she could ever remember. No sooner had she scrubbed the floor than she was told to go and work at her spinning by the mill pond.

'And don't let us catch sight of you,' her mother warned her, 'until you have teased out all the flax.'

The warm sun and the bright flowers on the bank made Greta feel less sad as she began her task. Then something

If she finished all her work for the afternoon, she was put to spinning.

dreadful happened! The spindle slipped from her hand and fell into the water.

Greta stared down into the dark deep water trying in vain to catch a glimpse of the lost spindle. And when she gave up hope at last of ever seeing it again, tears came to her eyes. What would her mother say? What cruel punishment would she be given for her carelessness?

How long she sat by the pond she did not know, but as she began walking slowly

Greta wept over the lost spindle.

homewards, she hoped that her mother and sister would not be there to greet her.

They were just leaving the house as she went up the garden path, and her mother said sharply, 'What brings you back so early?'

'I—I have lost the spindle,' Greta said in a trembling voice. 'It—it fell into the deep water of the mill pond and now it has gone for ever.'

'Fool!' cried her mother angrily, and Erica smiled spitefully. 'Tell her to jump in after it,' she giggled.

'Please don't ask me to do that!' the poor child exclaimed. 'I am truly sorry for what has happened.'

'Your sister is right,' her mother said with a cruel glint in her eyes. 'You must

'Go back to the pond and find the missing spindle at all costs.'

With a cry of despair she threw herself into the water.

go back to the pond and find the missing
spindle at all costs.'

So Greta ran back to the pond and with
a cry of despair threw herself into the
dark, uninviting water after her spindle.
Down, down, she sank until she lost all her

She was in a beautiful meadow of sweet-scented flowers.

senses. When she opened her eyes and was herself again, she found to her joy that she was in a beautiful meadow, and in the midst of sweet-scented flowers. Could this be paradise, she wondered, as she looked around her?

Presently she came upon a strange sight—a baker's oven full of bread. As she stared at it, the bread called, 'Take me out, take me out, before I am all scorched and burnt!' And Greta took the bread out of

'Take me out, take me out!' called the bread.

the hot oven and laid it carefully on the grass.

Soon after she came upon an apple tree laden with rosy red apples. 'Shake me, shake me!' the tree called to her. 'My apples are ripe!' And Greta went up to the tree and shook it until all its ripe apples tumbled to the ground.

She stopped by the tree long enough to gather the ripe apples into tidy heaps before hurrying on, for now she had a great wish to know what lay beyond the meadow.

She shook the tree until the apples fell.

A little house with crooked doors and tiny windows lay beyond the pretty meadow, and Greta ran towards it.

'Come in, child, and welcome to my little house,' an old woman called to her from an open window, and when Greta hung back shyly, she hobbled to the door and with a warm, friendly smile invited her inside.

*With a warm friendly smile
she invited Greta inside.*

'My name is Mother Holle,' the old dame said. 'You may stay here if you like and work for me. If you promise to make my bed and shake the pillows till the feathers fly, and do all the other work in the house, I will treat you kindly.'

'I promise,' said Greta, and that same day she ran upstairs and made the bed and shook the pillows until the feathers flew out of the window like snowflakes.

And when that was done, she tidied up the kitchen and made the soup.

She shook the pillows until the feathers flew like snowflakes.

Then she tidied the kitchen and made the soup.

'I long to see my mother and sister again. I want to go home,' said the girl.

As Greta stood in the doorway, a shower of golden rain fell upon her.

Greta worked so well and was so neat and tidy that the old woman never had to speak a cross word to her. Every day she gave Greta fish or meat for her dinner and showed her many small kindnesses, so the girl grew very fond of her.

But as the weeks passed, Greta could not help thinking of her own house. She had never been happy there, but still she was homesick. And so, one day, she said to Mother Holle, 'Please do not think that I am ungrateful but I long to see my mother and sister again. I want to go home.'

'Are you sure, child?' asked Mother Holle, looking sad. 'You have served me well, I shall be sad to see you go.'

'I am sure,' Greta said.

'Then I will take you up again my-self,' said the old woman.

'Let me make your bed once more and shake the pillows until the feathers fly,' said Greta. And she ran upstairs and made the old woman's bed for the last time.

Mother Holle was waiting for her in the kitchen and she took Greta's hand and led her to a great door. The door was open, and as Greta stood in the doorway, a shower of golden rain fell upon her.

Her old rags became a wonderful golden dress, and the gold stuck to her hair and her face and her arms, turning her into a golden girl.

'The gold is your reward for all your hard work,' Mother Holle smiled. 'Do not trouble your pretty head about the spindle. When they see the gold, they will forget all about it.' Then the great door closed and Greta found herself by the pond.

'Cock-a-doodle-doo!

Your golden girl's come back to you!' the handsome cockerel crowed as Greta ran back to the house.

Her mother and sister greeted her with gasps of amazement, and when she had told them her story, the widow said that Erica should enjoy the same good fortune as Greta.

'Go to the pond,' said her mother. 'Go this very day and throw one of the spindles into it. Then dive in after it. You will

'Cock-a-doodle-doo!
Your golden girl's come back to you!'

*They greeted her
with gasps of
amazement.*

come to no harm, for according to your sister this Mother Holle will be waiting to welcome you.'

Now Erica was so jealous of her sister that she took time only to find a spindle before running to the pond and throwing

Erica threw herself into the water after the spindle.

it in. Then she threw herself into the water after it.

As the water closed above her head, she lost all her senses. When she was herself again, she found she was in the same lovely meadow which Greta had told her

about. The pretty flowers did not interest Erica, for she was thinking about the gold that would soon be hers.

As she hurried across the meadow she came upon the baker's oven full of bread.

'Take me out, take me out before I am scorched and burnt!' the bread called.

Erica stared at the bread for a moment, then she exclaimed, 'Why should I take you out? You can scorch and burn until you are a cinder for all I care!'

And she ran on. When the baker's oven was left behind, she came upon the apple tree with its ripe, rosy red apples.

'Shake me! Shake me!' the tree called to her. 'My apples are ripe and ready to fall. Shake me! Shake me!'

Erica looked up at the rosy red apples

'Why should I take you out?' she said to the bread.

'I won't shake you, you silly old tree.'

and she thought to herself, 'I wouldn't mind eating one. But as for going to the bother of shaking the tree, why should I?'

And so the lazy girl answered, 'I won't shake you, you silly old tree. Anyway if I did, one of your apples might fall on my head!' And she ran on until she reached Mother Holle's crooked little house.

The old woman invited her inside with the words, 'You may stay here and work for me. But you must promise to make my bed and shake the pillows till the feathers fly and do all the other work properly.'

'I'll start right away,' said Erica, and she followed the old woman upstairs and set about making the bed. But, oh dear, lazy Erica had never made a bed in her life. She did not shake the pillows until all

Erica had never made a bed in her life.

feathers flew, and she did not smooth the sheets.

The old woman watched her in silence. Then she showed her a basket of linen and told her to wash it in the stream.

Now Erica had made up her mind to do everything that was asked of her. But she was so lazy and so disagreeable by nature that she soon stopped trying to please the old woman. She washed the clothes with so little care that the fine linen was soon torn and spoiled.

And so it was with all the other tasks she was asked to do, until by the end of the week she was not even bothering to rise at the proper time.

'I want to go home now,' she told the old dame one morning, and she thought of the shower of golden rain that would be presently falling upon her.

'Very well,' said Mother Holle, and she led her to the great door and told her to stand in the doorway.

'Now is the moment,' Erica thought. 'I am taller than Greta. More of the gold will stick to me!'

But as she stood there, a huge kettle of nasty sticky tar was emptied over her.

The linen she washed was soon torn and spoiled.

A huge kettle of nasty sticky tar was emptied over her.

'Now you are rewarded for the work you have done for me,' said Mother Holle, and she shut the great door.

Sobbing bitterly, Erica found herself by the pond, and as she ran towards her house, she heard the handsome cockerel crow:

'Cock-a-doodle-doo!
Your dirty girl's come back to you!'

Well, the nasty black tar stuck to Erica for many a year, and she and her mother had to live in a lonely part of the country, leaving their fine house to Greta—old Mother Holle's golden girl!

The Three Little Men in the Wood

There was once upon a time a man who had lost his wife, and a woman who had lost her husband. They lived in the same town close to a large wood.

Now the man whose wife had died had a very pretty daughter with big blue eyes and long golden hair. And the woman who had lost her husband had a very plain daughter with short dark hair that was so straight it stuck out like straw.

The two girls knew each other and were friends. One day the plain girl, whose name was Tinca, said to her pretty friend, 'My mother would like to marry again. She would like to marry your father.'

'I don't know about that,' said her friend, shaking her head.

'She says that she will be specially kind to you,' said Tinca. 'She says that she will see to it that you wash in milk every morning and even have wine to drink instead of water.'

'What about you?' asked the pretty girl. 'What will she do for you?'

'Oh, she doesn't promise anything like that for me,' came the reply. 'I shall just have to wash in water as usual, and drink water at meal-times. Will you tell your father what she says?'

So the gentle fair-haired girl went to her father. 'If you marry the widow,' she said, 'she has promised to treat me well. She says I will bathe in milk every day and drink wine at meal-times. What do you say, father? Is it a good idea?'

'I will have to think about it,' said the widower. 'A second marriage does not always turn out well.'

The widower thought about the widow's proposal all day, and when still he could not make up his mind, he said to his daughter, 'Take this old boot of mine and hang it up in the attic. It has a hole in the sole. Pour water into it and if the hole closes up and the boot holds the water— then I will marry the widow!'

'And if it does not hold the water?' his daughter asked.

'It will be a sign that I should not marry again,' said her father.

So then the girl took the old boot into the attic and hung it up. Then she poured a kettle of water into it and, lo and behold, the hole closed up and the boot held the water.

'Father, father!' she cried, rushing down the stairs. 'The old boot is holding the water!'

'I will marry the widow,' her father declared. 'She and her daughter can live here in this house.'

The marriage between the widower and the widow was quickly arranged and after it had taken place the widow and her plain daughter moved into the widower's house.

The next day when the pretty golden-haired girl went to bathe she found a tub of milk specially prepared for her by her new stepmother, and that night at supper she was given wine to drink.

The widow's own daughter, however, had to wash in water and had only water to drink at meal-times.

'Your mother has kept her promise,' the pretty girl whispered to her friend. 'She is very good to me.'

Alas, the stepmother soon began to show her dislike for the daughter of her new husband. And by the end of the week the poor girl found that she must wash in icy cold water and drink water at every meal. She was given all the hardest work in the house to do and was for ever being scolded by the stepmother.

'She has turned against you,' Tinca said one morning. 'Now she is spoiling

The two little girls were friends.

Mother and daughter bullied the girl.

me with attention. Now I am the one to wash in milk and have wine.'

'Why has this happened?' her friend asked tearfully.

'It is because you are so pretty,' Tinca told her. 'My mother is angry with you because you are much prettier than I am. She cannot forgive you for that!' And she laughed spitefully for she too had grown envious of her new sister.

All that summer mother and daughter bullied the pretty girl and thought up ways to make her unhappy. And when winter came, the mother made a dress out of paper for the golden-haired child and forced her to put it on.

The winter that year was particularly hard. On a freezing cold day the woman told her stepdaughter to go into the wood with her basket and find her some of the wild strawberries which grew there in the

One day she was sent into the wood wearing her paper dress.

summer. In her heart she hoped that the girl would die out there in the snow, for her paper dress would be no protection against the cold.

The girl began searching the woods for the wild strawberries but, of course, she found none. Instead she came upon a little house in the middle of the wood.

Three little men peeped at her from one of its windows and the girl waved and asked if she might enter.

'Yes, come in,' they cried. And the girl

She came upon a little house in the middle of the wood.

'Why are you out in the woods on such a day and wearing only a dress made of paper?'

went in and sat down beside a blazing stove.

'Have you anything you can share with us?' one of the little men asked after some minutes.

'I have nothing,' said the girl, 'except a slice of stale bread which my stepmother gave me for my breakfast.'

'Will you share it with us?' asked the second little man.

'Willingly,' said the girl, and she broke the bread into four pieces, keeping the smallest piece for herself.

When the bread had been eaten, the third little man said, 'Why are you out in the woods on such a day and wearing only a dress made of paper?'

'I am searching for wild strawberries,' the girl said. 'I dare not return home until I have found some.'

173

'Before you leave us,' said the first of the little men, 'would you do something for us?'

'Of course,' said the pretty girl. 'I will do anything you ask.'

'Then take a broom and sweep the snow away from the house,' said the second little man. And he smiled up at her.

As soon as the girl went outside to sweep the snow away, the three little men seated themselves on the top step of their house and watched her.

'She is kind and gentle,' said the first.

'She is generous too,' said the second.

'What presents shall we give her then?' demanded the third.

'I will see to it that she finds a clump of wild strawberries,' said the first.

'I will see to it that she is showered with gold coins as soon as she speaks,' said the second.

'I will see to it that a king falls in love with her,' said the third.

The three little men sat and watched her as she swept away the snow.

With her basket brimming over with the fruit she set off for home.

The first of the little men's wishes for the pretty girl soon came true for, as she cleared the snow, she came upon a patch of wild strawberries, and with a cry of joy ran to show them to her new friends.

Then with her basket brimming over with the fruit, she set off for home.

Her wicked stepmother and her spiteful stepsister were so angry and disappointed at seeing her again that they

176

paid not the slightest attention to the strawberries. They began scolding her for taking such a long time over her task.

As the poor girl began to explain about the three little men in the wood, a shower of gold coins fell at her feet.

'These three little men must be wizards!' exclaimed the astonished step-mother. 'If they can do this for you, they

As she began to explain a shower of gold coins fell at her feet.

She was dressed in soft white furs and in her basket was a piece of delicious fruit cake.

can do it for my own dear child!' And turning to Tinca she told her that she too must visit the little house in the middle of the wood.

The very next morning Tinca set off. She was richly and warmly dressed in soft white furs and in her basket was a piece of delicious fruit cake.

She struggled through the deep snow until she came to the little house and there at the window were the faces of the three little men. But she did not wave them a friendly greeting. Instead she stamped into the kitchen and sat down by the blazing stove.

'Have you anything to share with us?' asked one of the little men.

'I have a piece of fruit cake,' Tinca said. 'But I am hungry and I intend to eat it all myself—so there!'

After she had eaten her cake, she stared at the three little men hopefully, thinking they would give her the wild strawberries. But one of them asked if she would be kind enough to sweep away the snow.

'Goodness me!' Tinca cried. 'What do you take me for? Sweep the snow away from the steps if you want to—but don't ask me!' And she went outside to look for the wild strawberries herself.

'She is rude and selfish,' said the first little man, as he crossed to the window to watch her.

'She is mean and greedy,' said the second, as he joined his companion.

'What shall we give her?' asked the third, also going to the window. 'What do you say to a few toads to keep her company when she gets home?'

She went outside to look for the wild strawberries.

*She set off through the woods
with her empty basket.*

The others chuckled and agreed and presently, when Tinca failed to find the strawberries, they nodded and winked at each other as they saw her set off through the woods with her empty basket.

Stumbling through the deep snow was so unpleasant that when Tinca arrived home she was in a very bad temper.

She threw off her expensive furs and, as her mother ran to greet her, she shouted angrily, 'It was a useless journey! I didn't find any wild strawberries and those three little men were horrid to me!'

But her mother and the servants scarcely took in what she was saying. They were all staring at the four big toads which were hopping around her feet.

'So that's all you managed to get out of the little men in the wood!' her angry, disappointed mother cried at last. 'Well, I expect that mealy-mouthed stepsister of yours persuaded them to play this mean

They were all staring at the four big toads which were hopping around her feet.

trick on you. Don't fret, Tinca, I will see that she pays for it!'

And the next day the stepmother sent her stepdaughter down to the duck pond with a bundle of linen.

'Take this hammer and break the ice with it,' she ordered. 'And then wash the linen in the water,' she went on. And she

hoped the girl would catch her death of cold.

Clad only in her working dress and with no shoes on her feet the girl set off for

The next day she was sent down to the duck pond with a bundle of linen.

the pond which was frozen over with a thick layer of ice.

As she began to break the ice with the hammer, the young king of a neighbouring land came riding by in his coach.

When he saw the pretty, golden-haired girl striking the ice with the heavy hammer, he was moved to pity.

'How lovely she is!' he thought, and he ordered his coachman to stop. Then he left the coach and went over to speak to the girl whose lot, he felt, must be a sad one.

As soon as he had heard her story, he

As she began to break the ice with her hammer the young king of a neighbouring kingdom came riding by in his coach.

He asked her to ride back to his palace with him.

They drove off through the snow to his palace.

took her cold hands in his and asked her to ride back to his palace with him.

'There is no sweeter girl in the whole of my kingdom,' said he. 'If you will return with me, I give you my word that we shall be married.'

The pretty girl did not hesitate. 'I will go with you, sire,' she said. 'My life is so miserable at home that I have no wish to return there.'

And she followed the young handsome king to his coach. When they were seated, side by side, the coachman cracked his whip and the splendid pair of white horses moved off through the snow.

When they arrived at the palace, the king was as good as his word. With all

The stepmother and her daughter went to visit the young king and queen.

haste he made arrangements for his wedding, and the girl, more beautiful than ever in her wedding dress of smooth white satin became his queen.

In every way the marriage was a happy one, and when a year had passed, the queen bore a son, which so delighted her young husband that he arranged for a month's celebrations to be held throughout the land.

News of the great good fortune of her stepdaughter came to the ears of the wicked mother, and she determined to go to the palace and see for herself how best she could take her revenge.

'Don't you fret or be jealous of her,' the woman said to her own daughter. 'You must come with me to the palace, and when we get there we must pretend to be pleased that she has found happiness.'

So the disagreeable pair set out for the palace and when they arrived, they were shown into the presence of the young king and queen.

'Let the past be forgotten,' said the mother. 'Tinca and I have come to pay our respects to you.'

The young queen was only too happy to forget the evil her stepmother had done to her, and as she began talking about her baby son, as fond mothers will, the king left the party to go hunting.

No sooner was he gone than the wicked woman snatched the baby from the queen

She sent him away, saying his young queen was sound asleep.

and put him in his cradle. Then, with Tinca's help, she took hold of the slender young queen and tossed her out of the window and into the stream which flowed beneath.

'Quick!' she cried to Tinca. 'Jump into her bed and I will cover your face!'

'I will tell him that his young wife has a fever and must not be disturbed,' she said. 'And in time he will forget all about that wretched girl he now loves.'

The king did not appear until late that night and the woman sent him away with soft words, saying his young queen was sound asleep and should not be disturbed.

Early the next morning, long before most of the palace servants were awake, the king's young page boy was out walking by the stream unable to sleep for tooth-ache. As he sat by the bank to rest, a little white duck swam up to him and said, 'What do my guests do?'

And the boy answered, 'They are fast asleep as far as I know.'

Then the duck said, 'What does my little babe do?'

And the boy answered, 'The royal child is asleep in his cradle.'

Then the duck took the shape of the young queen and left the stream and went

'What does my little babe do?' the duck asked the page boy.

into the palace to the nursery where she picked up her child and loved him for a moment before going back to the stream where once again she took the form of a duck.

The page boy said nothing of this to the king but he kept watch over the little duck and was present when once again, the next morning, it took the shape of the queen. On the third morning the duck said, 'Go and tell the king to wait for my spirit as it enters the palace. Tell him he must take his sword and wave it over me three times. Beg him not to fail.'

Gladly the young page boy ran to his master and told him all he had seen and what the little duck had said.

The king was at first amazed and then angry, but he believed what the page boy had told him. When next the spirit of his lovely young queen entered the palace, he was there with his sword. And as he waved it above her head, the spirit became his own flesh-and-blood wife.

Then she told him what her wicked stepmother had done and the king vowed that he would have his revenge.

Later that day he went to the old woman who sat by Tinca's heavily curtained bed. 'Ah,' said he, with a smile, 'I have heard a sorry tale of a man who threw another out of the window. Now I have come to ask you for your advice as to his punishment.'

'Oh,' cried the wicked woman without thinking. 'If I were king I would put him in a barrel, and roll him down the hill into the water . . .'

'Woman!' thundered the king, 'you have sentenced yourself. That will be your punishment for your evil deeds.'

So that was the end of the jealous mother—and her ugly daughter, for she too shared the same fate.

The queen sent the three little men in the wood an invitation to her baby's christening, but strange to say, she did not hear from them, then, or ever again!

She left the stream and went into the palace to the nursery.

The Little Mermaid

Once upon a time there was a beautiful little mermaid who lived with her father and her five sisters at the bottom of the sea.

Now you must not imagine that it was black and frightening in the ocean's depth. It was just the opposite. The little mermaid was the daughter of the Mer-king, and the palace in which she grew up was a splendid one. It was built of red and white coral, and through its many windows little fishes, some a delicate pale green and others a bright red and blue, would swim in and out. They were as much at home in the palace as they were among the rocks and the dark sea caves.

In the gardens surrounding the Mer-king's palace were the most gorgeous sea plants and trailing flowers which were a joy to gaze upon. The little mermaid loved the flowers especially, and she and her five sisters had gardens of their own which they decorated with glowing pebbles and all manner of entrancing colourful sea shells.

The mermaids had no mother, but they did have a grandmother—a handsome old Mer-lady whose tender care for her grandchildren was rewarded by their love.

The royal grandmother ruled the palace with a firm but kindly hand. And the Mer-king considered her so important that he granted her one of the highest honours. She, alone, was allowed to decorate her tail with oyster shells!

All the Mer-princesses were extremely beautiful, but the little mermaid, who was the youngest, had the prettiest hair—it was golden rather than reddish-brown—and the bluest eyes.

The grandmother cared for the little mermaid more than her sisters. This was not because she was prettier but because she was so quiet and gentle. And, it must be admitted, because she was so eager to hear the old lady's stories!

Day after day the little mermaid would beg her grandmother to tell her of the world above the sea.

'You say they do not have tails like ours!' she would remark in her soft, gentle voice. 'How very strange that seems! Oh, how I long to see these human beings for myself.'

And then her grandmother would tell her, as she had told her many times before, that she would not be permitted to leave the coral palace and swim freely in the blue sea until she was fifteen years old.

'Be patient, child,' the old lady would say kindly. 'Your time will come!'

But the little mermaid found it hard to be patient. She thought so much about the strange beings who lived above the sea that she even neglected her garden.

Then one day her sisters gave her a present for her garden and from that moment onwards the little mermaid spent all her free time there.

Their present was a strange one. It was a beautiful white marble statue of a young boy. It had come from a ship, wrecked at sea not far from their palace, and the five sisters had brought it home.

Day after day the youngest princess sat in her garden, staring at the statue and dreaming of the day when she would be old enough to find out for herself what real men and women would be like.

'How much longer must I wait?' she

Day after day the princess sat in her garden staring at the statue.

'Soon you will be fifteen,' said her grandmother.

asked her grandmother one morning as she set out to visit the statue. 'All my sisters have now been allowed to go above the sea—I am the only one who doesn't know what it is like.'

'The Mer-king's law cannot be broken,' said her grandmother patiently. 'You have not much longer to wait, for soon you will be fifteen.'

The little mermaid sighed as she sat down beside her grandmother. It was so hard to be patient!

'Ask your sisters to tell you again of the wonders they have seen above our blue sea,' the old lady said at last, after a long silence. 'Do not spend so much of your time dreaming in front of that boy-statue they gave you. Try and be more like them! They are always so gay . . .'

'You are right,' said the little princess. 'I will seek them out and ask them to talk to me of the other world.'

That day the little mermaid did not visit her garden. She went searching for her sisters. And when she found them she begged them to tell her all they had seen when they left home.

'So our little sister has time for us at last,' teased the eldest. 'Let me tell you what I did when I rose above the sea. I sat upon a sandbank in the moonlight and watched what happened in the town built along the shore. I saw men—they walked on two legs just like our grandmother said they would—and I saw many dull grey houses and high church towers from which came the sound of bells.'

'Is that all?' asked the little mermaid. 'Oh—not all,' said her eldest sister. 'But here is much nicer, I promise you.'

'Now tell me what you saw!' the little mermaid exclaimed, turning to the next of her sisters.

'But I did tell you!' protested her sister. 'Perhaps you were too young to listen properly. Well, when I rose to the surface of the sea, the sun was just setting, and the sky was so very beautiful that I could scarcely take my eyes away from it. Then I saw a flock of white swans and they too were beautiful—as beautiful as any of our fishes.'

'Was there more?' asked the little mermaid.

'I don't think so,' said her sister. 'I was quite tired when I came back but it was all great fun, you know.'

'I remember I swam into a bay where some children were playing,' said the third sister. 'I heard the birds singing in the wood which fringed the bay. But it was the children I liked.'

'What happened? Did you try to speak to them?' the little mermaid asked with an eager smile for she was thinking of her boy-statue.

'I wanted to play with them,' said her sister, 'as they swam about in the sea. But I must have frightened them, for they all swam away from me as fast as they could.'

'Well, I didn't see any humans,' said the fourth sister. 'I didn't venture very far. I just saw some fine sailing ships and some pretty sea gulls in the sky. If you ask me, it is much nicer under the sea with all our friends.'

'I don't agree with you,' said the fifth sister. 'When I went to the surface, it was winter. I saw giant icebergs chasing men in ships. It was very exciting and I sat on one of the icebergs until the night-clouds covered the sky.'

'I shall be fifteen in the spring,' said the little mermaid. 'I won't see any giant icebergs.'

'You will be free to go to the surface any time you choose once you are fifteen,' her eldest sister said.

That evening the five sisters, because they had talked so much about the world above, joined hands and rose to the surface, singing sweet, haunting songs as they circled the ships.

Left alone in the palace, the youngest mermaid was ready to weep, so much did she long to be with them. But mermaids

*She swam upwards until she found herself rising
out of a sea that was as smooth as glass.*

cannot shed tears, and so she remained
dry-eyed and miserable, waiting for their
return.

Slowly the time passed, and then one
day it was her birthday and she was fifteen
years old! Her grandmother put a garland
of white sea flowers on her head as a token
of her new rank.

'Do not be disappointed if the world
above us is not as beautiful as you wished
it to be,' said the old lady.

'I won't,' promised the little mermaid,
trembling with excitement. And she
swam upwards until she found herself
rising out of a sea that was as smooth as
glass.

The little mermaid's blue eyes shone
with pleasure as she looked up and saw
above her the night sky lit by a hundred
twinkling stars. And she thought, 'My
dream of the world is coming true. This
is the sky they see. My sisters said the sky

was beautiful but they did not tell me about the stars.'

Then she saw, some distance away, a great ship lying at anchor, with only one white sail unfurled. Sailors were moving about the deck, and there was the sound of music and men's laughter.

The little mermaid swam nearer to the great ship. She went so close that she could peer into one of its lighted cabins and there she saw a tall, elegant young man. He was richly dressed and there was a golden crown embroidered on his robe.

'He must be a prince,' she said to herself. 'Only a prince would have such a noble bearing!'

It was growing late, but the little mermaid could not bear to leave the ship or cease watching the handsome prince. But then the sea, which a moment before had been so smooth and friendly, became suddenly fiercely angry.

The little mermaid knew and understood the sea and was not afraid. She saw its huge, raging waves strike the ship's side and sweep over her decks.

She heard the shouts of the sailors, who were not prepared for the storm, and she swam away from the stricken vessel.

But she could not bear to leave the prince, and so she waited to see how the royal ship would weather the tempest.

The ship struggled bravely against the battering waves for a time and the little mermaid began to hope that the skill of the sailors would save her.

Then, as the wind reached gale force, the sea surged in and the men let out a desperate cry of fear. It was just as if a giant hand had taken hold of their beautiful ship and was forcing her over on her side. She listed dangerously, and then began to sink.

In their terror the men aboard her jumped into the raging sea and the little mermaid searched for her prince among the drowning crew.

She saw him at last and she saw how weakly he was swimming.

'He will sink to the ocean's bed,' she thought, 'and then he will be mine for ever!'

Suddenly something her grandmother had told her made her terribly afraid for the young man. She had said that if a human fell into the sea and could not swim he would be lost for ever.

'I must save him,' the little mermaid

The little mermaid held the prince in her arms.

told herself. And she swam quickly to him, cradling his head in her arms, as she pulled him away from the wreck.

For the rest of that night the little mermaid held the prince in her arms. His eyes were closed and he scarcely seemed to breathe, but she stroked his face and kissed his hair as she kept him above the water. And the current drew them steadily towards land.

By morning the storm had passed, and the sea was calm and friendly again. But it had claimed the ship and the crew for there was no sign of them.

The loss of the beautiful ship did not concern the little mermaid; she had

She swam with him to the shore.

thoughts only for the prince. When she saw that they were now in some kind of deep bay she knew she had saved him.

She swam with him to the shore and laid him gently on the warm, firm sand. And she kissed him once again and begged him to open his eyes and speak to her.

But the prince did not open his eyes or make any sign that he was alive and the little mermaid grew afraid for him and wished that some other humans would come and help to save him.

Presently, from the little white chapel, which stood beyond the fringe of trees, came the sound of a bell ringing, and a

One of the girls saw the young man lying on the sand.

group of pretty young girls came out of the little church.

One of them saw the young man lying on the sand and as she ran towards him the little mermaid, terror-stricken in case she was seen, hid behind a large rock.

She watched, wide-eyed, as the girl stared down at the prince for a startled moment and then shouted to her friends to come and help her.

The little mermaid sighed with relief as the girl, with the aid of her friends, carried the young prince to their house.

As they passed the rock where she lay hidden, the prince opened his eyes for an instant and smiled.

'He thinks it is they who saved his life,' the little mermaid told herself mournfully. 'But what does that matter? He is alive!' And she made her way to the water's edge and plunged into the sea. She had been away from home for many hours and her grandmother, especially, would be growing anxious about her.

The little mermaid had always been quiet and thoughtful, but now she grew so quiet and showed so clearly that her joy was to sit before the marble boy-statue that her grandmother and her sisters were concerned for her.

'Why does she refuse to tell us what she saw when she visited the world above?' one of the sisters asked her grandmother.

'You must ask her,' said the wise old lady. 'If you ask her directly she will tell you.'

So the eldest of the sisters asked the little mermaid to confide in her.

'The statue reminds me of a prince I saved from the sea's fury,' said the little mermaid, with a heavy sigh. 'I think of him all the time, but I do not know where he lives . . .'

'But I know!' cried the eldest sister, pleased to be of help. 'We heard stories of the wreck and how the prince aboard her was found on the golden sands of the bay. Come, I know where his palace stands. It is large and yellow with steps running straight down to the sea.'

'Will you take me to it now?' asked the little mermaid, suddenly alive with excitement and eagerness.

'Of course,' said her sister, and she took the little mermaid by the hand and swam with her until it was time to rise out of the water. There in front of them was the palace.

She was so full of joy at having found where her beloved lived.

The little mermaid left her sister and rested for a moment on the marble steps. She was so full of joy at having found where her beloved prince lived that she could not speak. It was enough to gaze up at the fine palace and think about him, and wish him happiness.

After that first visit the little mermaid went many times to the golden palace. Sometimes, on bright moonlit nights, when the prince thought he was alone, the little mermaid stole up quite close to him as he sat on the sea wall.

At other times she watched him from a distance as he sailed his boat or dived from the high rocks.

There were days and nights when the prince did not appear and the little mermaid became sad and downcast. And then her sisters would try to make her smile as they told her stories they had overhead from the fishermen. These were stories about the prince—how brave he was, how kind and thoughtful he was at home, and how all his subjects loved him dearly.

'Does a human have to die?' the mermaid asked her grandmother one day.

'Yes,' came the reply. 'We go on living for three hundred years and then we become foam on the sea. Human beings have souls which go on living for ever—even though their bodies die and turn to dust. But then they live only a short time compared to us.'

'I wish I could be a human being,' sighed the little mermaid, thinking of her prince.

'That is a foolish wish,' said the grand old lady sharply. 'If it came true you would not have a soul unless you found a human man who loved you with all his heart. Then it is possible you might be given a part of his soul.'

The little mermaid sighed again as she said, 'Humans walk on two funny things they call legs. Could they possibly love us Mer-people who only have long scaly tails?'

'Of course not!' exclaimed her grandmother. 'But our long scaly tails are much more beautiful than legs . . .'

The little mermaid thought much about what her grandmother had said and she began to long to have legs like her prince.

At last she made up her mind to pay a visit to the sea-witch, whose home was by a deep, dark whirlpool far away from the red and white coral palace and beautiful gardens. To reach it she must pass through dreadful black, slimy swamps where the sea-witch kept her serpents and monster toads.

It was a truly terrifying journey and when at last the little mermaid stood before the old witch she was still trembling.

'Help me mother-witch,' she began in a weak, frightened voice. 'Help me to gain my heart's desire. I want to rid myself of my tail and have in its place two legs, the kind humans use for walking.'

'I know the reason for this foolish wish,' said the old sea-witch with a shrill, cruel laugh. 'You have fallen in love with a prince. You want him to love you and share his immortal soul with you.'

'Yes, that is true,' the princess admitted.

'Are you prepared to endure the most terrible suffering?' the witch demanded, as she stirred the bubbling mixture in her

The witch filled her kettle-spoon with the potion and held it out to her.

cauldron. 'Are you ready to turn to foam if you fail to win the prince's love?'

'I am ready,' whispered the mermaid.

And the witch filled her kettle-spoon with some of the steaming potion and held it out to the princess. 'Three drops of this will change your tail to the props men call legs,' she told her.

'But I must not drink it now, the little mermaid protested. 'I must first swim to his palace.'

'I will pour the magic potion into a phial,' said the sea-witch. 'Drink it when you reach the palace. And now I will take your sweet voice in payment.'

And she cut out the little mermaid's tongue, leaving her dumb and speechless. Then she gave her the phial and with a cruel smile sent her on her way.

The sun had not yet risen when the little mermaid arrived at the prince's palace. She pulled herself out of the water and over the sea wall. Then she sipped the magic liquid in the phial.

Pain as keen as the sharpest knife pierced the little mermaid's body, and she lay down at the foot of the marble steps and closed her eyes.

How long she lay there she did not know, but when at last she stirred it was to find the young prince kneeling at her side. Covering her with his cloak, he began asking her who she was and how she came to be lying there.

'Never have I seen a maid so lovely!' the prince declared, and he put out a gentle hand to stroke the little mermaid's long golden hair.

The little mermaid gazed up at him, speechless, and her blue eyes were so bright and loving that the young man was suddenly at a loss for words.

'Did you come from the sea?' he asked finally. 'Was some ship perhaps wrecked on the rocks?'

And when the girl still did not answer, the prince helped her to rise. As she stood, slim and straight on her two legs, it was as if she were standing on nails. How right the witch had been! The pain was dreadful, but the little mermaid gave no sign of her suffering.

The prince showed his surprise as the beautiful young girl moved towards the

*She awoke to find the young prince kneeling at
her side and covering her with his cloak.*

marble steps. She moved with the grace
of an angel and he stared at her, fascinated
by her airy lightness. Then he hurried her
into the palace where he called some of his
mother's ladies-in-waiting to come to him.

'See that my guest has all the clothes
she requires,' he ordered.

So the little mermaid was robed in
rich dresses of silk and muslin and she was
so delicately lovely and so clearly eager to

please that she became a great favourite
with the prince. But she could neither
speak nor sing and this often made her sad.

She saw how the prince loved music
and how the pretty court ladies were able
to please him with their singing.

'Once I had the sweetest voice in the
Mer-kingdom,' she thought sadly.

But then one day two of the most
beautiful of the slave girls danced for their

royal master. The little mermaid saw the pleasure on his face as he watched them and when they had gone, she rose to her feet and started to dance.

So light was she and so graceful that she was like thistledown blown this way and that by the softest of breezes. And the prince and all those watching were quite entranced by her movements.

The prince especially was completely enraptured, and when she ceased, he called out, 'More, more, my little one.'

Every step caused the little mermaid the most terrible suffering, but the pain was nothing compared to her joy at knowing she was pleasing her prince. And she began dancing again.

When the prince decided that she had danced long enough, he summoned her to his side, and began talking to her in a low, kindly voice.

'I want you always by my side,' he said. 'From now on you shall be my constant little companion and friend. When I go out riding, you shall come with me. When I retire at night you shall sleep on a velvet cushion in my own apartments.'

The mermaid's blue eyes glowed with love at this and she longed to tell the prince all that was in her heart. But she could only smile.

The next day she went riding with the prince, and he talked to her of the beauty of the woods and of the pleasure he had in listening to the sweet songs of the birds. And the little mermaid smiled and nodded, longing to hear him speak of the love he felt for herself.

But the young prince did not speak of love, only of friendship and of the joy he found at being in her company.

That night the little mermaid stole down to the water's edge. As she stood in the cool soothing water to ease her aching feet she thought of her father, the Merking, and of her grandmother and her five sisters.

'If only I could see them again,' she told herself. 'I would be able to make them understand why I had to leave them.'

One night, some weeks later, she did see her five sisters again. They rose out of the water and called a greeting to her, and the little mermaid told them about her love for the prince and how she could not leave him—not even though she missed her home and the love of her family.

'We will tell our father,' said the eldest. 'He mourns you as if you were already turned to foam. Have courage, little sister, we shall come when we can to speak with you and give you news.'

Soon after she had seen her sisters, the prince took her climbing and as they sat together on the highest peak of the mountain the little mermaid looked at the young man with questioning eyes. Was this the moment when at last he would tell her how much he had come to love her?

But the prince did not look upon his faithful companion as a possible bride. He thought of her only as his dear little sister. And so, without any idea of how much he was hurting her, he began to speak of the plans his parents had made to find him a suitable wife.

'They say they have already found me a beautiful princess,' he said lightly. 'By all accounts she has a sweet nature as well. But then we shall soon find out what she is really like for tomorrow we set sail for her kingdom. And you, of course, will accompany us.'

Early next morning the prince and his

party boarded the royal ship. And the little mermaid hid her suffering and smiled whenever the prince turned to her.

But that night, when the prince and his friends were sound asleep in their cabins, the little mermaid went on deck, and the silver moon shone down on her sad face as she thought of what would happen to her.

Then somewhere out at sea she heard the gentle, whispering voices of her five sisters. 'If the prince marries another,' the eldest called, 'we will go at once to the sea-witch and ask her help.'

The silver moon shone down on her sad face.

The meeting between the beautiful princess and the handsome young prince took place the next day, and only those with dull eyes and leaden hearts failed to note that, for these two young people, it was no less than love at first sight. And the prince proclaimed his intentions of marrying the princess on the morrow.

After the wedding the royal party made its merry way back to the ship and, as night fell, the little mermaid once again found herself alone on deck.

She was so sad at the thought of all she had lost that not even the voices of her sisters calling to her from the sea could rouse her. But then the eldest, rising up out of the waves, cried, 'We have been to the witch. She has taken our long hair in exchange for this knife. Kill the prince with it. If you do, you will save yourself.'

The mermaid accepted the knife. She found the prince asleep when she reached his cabin and in his dreams he spoke his bride's name. As she heard it, the little mermaid threw down the fatal knife and, rushing up on deck, plunged into the sea.

But she did not, as she expected, turn to foam. Almost at once she was caught up in the strong arms of the wind.

Far below she saw the prince come out on deck to search for her and she had time to blow him a warm, fragrant kiss before the wind carried her far away to a new home in the starry heavens.

Almost at once she was caught up in the strong arms of the wind.